D0918839

DISCARD

Best Laid Plans

By the same author

Eight Days at The New Grand
Olivia's Garden
The Cuckoo's Nest
Return to Rosemount
Emily's Wedding
Family Secrets
A Perfect Mother
Rumours and Red Roses
Just Another Day
A Small Fortune

Best Laid Plans

Patricia Fawcett

ROBERT HALE · LONDON

First published in Great Britain 2013

ISBN 978 0 7198 1001 5

Robert Hale Limited
Clerkenwell House
Clerkenwell Green
London EC1R 0HT

www.halebooks.com

2 4 6 8 10 9 7 5 3 1

Typeset in New Century Schoolbook
Printed by TJ International, UK

PART ONE

Chapter One

Snape House,
Downill-by-Lune,
Lancashire.

Both of us would like to wish you a Happy Christmas!
We have had a good year and Frank is recovering well from a little health scare, although retirement is still a long way off. He keeps moving the goalposts as far as that is concerned. I have stopped helping out in the office and am enjoying the quiet life. Mike and darling Monique are very happy together and Amy is still running the world! She's at the top of her game in the retail trade and now has a senior job with the Leeds store and she has a beautiful flat in a Victorian house on the outskirts of town. You know Amy, she has no time for a significant relationship but that doesn't worry her at all. She's a career girl through and through.
Frank and I visit her whenever we can. We see much more of Mike and Monique, of course, who live down in the village. Mike is enjoying shadowing his father and will be ready to take over when the time comes and Monique is having some

success with her paintings. She is such a talented artist and beautiful with it and she certainly deserves it.
We hope you and yours are all well. Once again you are very welcome to pop in if you are in this part of the world. We have masses of room and would be delighted to see you.

Our very best wishes for the New Year

Christine and Frank Fletcher

Amy Fletcher, contrary to her mother's inflated expectations, did not quite run the department store.

But, considering she was only in her mid-thirties, she was reasonably happy with what might be considered to be a meteoric rise within the company. She was relishing the experience just now of working with Daniel Coleridge, an energetic man with an engaging smile who could have had another career as a young George Clooney look-alike. They had worked together before and she felt comfortable with him, pleased that their relationship was strictly business and therefore devoid of complications. Daniel had gained a reputation in the retail trade as an ideas man, a man of sure instincts with incredible trouble-shooting abilities and she was his right-hand woman, the one he bounced ideas off, the person who sorted out his brilliant, if sometimes chaotic, thoughts.

Their arrival at this store several months earlier was not entirely welcome, for Daniel's reputation had preceded his appointment and there had been a lot of huffing and puffing from the senior staff here, all of them nervous as hell, as well they might be. They had been coasting happily for years failing to see the danger signs that were flashing from every corner, blaming the store's decline on everything and everybody except themselves.

Affable as Daniel might be he was ruthless with it, and Amy admired that. It was unwise to underestimate him and after a couple of years of working together it suited them both that they did not meet outside the office. They were a good team and tried their damnedest to be firm but fair, although she knew they were considered by some to be the Bonnie and Clyde of the retail world, bursting in as they did and cutting a swathe through the hangers-on and the no-hopers.

Sadly, in business there is no place for sentiment, although that did not stop her from fretting every single time numbers were dangled in front of them, numbers that had to be sliced. Thankfully, more often than not, it could be achieved without too much heartache; old-timers were usually more than happy to snatch what they could and make a run for it. She knew for sure that Daniel would be moving on before long, for she was aware of the surreptitious approaches from rival companies but he had asked her to keep quiet and she was doing just that.

Wearing a pale blue blouse today with her dark grey suit – knee-length pencil skirt, neat fitted jacket – Amy hurried into their office to find Daniel's secretary Janet engaged in chatting with Bea from perfumery. Bea had a keen mind behind her blonde, blue-eyed model-like exterior and, at nearly six feet tall with the longest legs this side of the West End stage was as far removed from Amy as it was possible to be. Even though she was in no way petite herself, Amy still had to look up to her and it was doubly annoying that Bea could even make the workaday suit she was wearing look sexy. Just one look and Bea had set her sights on Daniel, who was blissfully unaware of it. He was young for the job, only six years older than Amy; he had been recruited by the big boss at head office himself and was held in high regard by him. He kept his private life private but he had let slip that he was divorced and off women, or at the least a serious relationship, forever so it would seem that Bea was wasting her energy on him. However, trying to look at it from a neutral viewpoint Amy saw that Bea working on full flirt power would be hard for any normal hot-blooded male to resist.

The two women stopped chatting when they saw Amy, smiles frozen, which made her wonder if they had been discussing her. The suspicion with which most of the staff regarded Daniel stretched to her, too, and it was amusing that they thought of her as some sort of internal spy. They were facing strong competition in the high street and needed to up their game and introduce the store to a much younger audience, which was why the basement area was at present undergoing a serious restructuring, the promised disco-like atmosphere and coffee bar intended to entice the youngsters in. It would be a no-go area for their older clientele, of course, but that was understood.

Langdales occupied a prime corner position in a busy shopping street. The windows had been beautifully dressed this festive season. Daniel had been responsible for that, stopping a dubious attempt to save on costs by spending a lot of money on new sparkly decorations. That old chestnut about having to spend money to make money was one of his mantras.

The result was that the store had never looked so good. It was like a lighthouse shining at the corner of the drab and dismal December street, a haven for tired and grumpy shoppers, a silvery glittery spectacle and up on the second floor Santa's grotto was an Arctic wonderland and this year, after a few complaints the previous one, they had hired a trio of men to do the Santa shifts, a jovial three who at least looked like the man himself.

Just now, using the stairs to get up to the offices – her token keep-fit trip of the day – Amy allowed herself a moment's satisfaction at the hordes of bustling shoppers that had squeezed in on this final Saturday before Christmas. They did not look particularly happy but then who in their right mind did at this crucial late stage of the Christmas buying spree? Mind you, whether or not they were actually buying or just looking would come out later.

'I've left last week's figures with Janet, Amy,' Bea told her, her tongue flicking over perfectly applied red lipstick. She was about a foot taller than Janet who was looking up at her with something approaching awe. 'It's been mayhem, utter pandemonium. We've had a fantastic run with "Bella-Sophia". They've been practically killing each other for the last few bottles. We're the only stockists in town and we could have sold it at double the price. The higher you price a perfume the better and that TV advert of theirs was a stroke of genius. Every woman wants to look like that, not to mention having that gorgeous hunk drooling over her.'

'Quite.' Amy caught the look Bea gave her, sympathetic verging on despair so that she had to bite her lip to check back an apology for letting standards slip and not looking her best today. She was at least two sizes larger than Bea but she thought – and she hoped it was not just wishful thinking – she could carry it off. The truth was she had been running round in circles since arriving here at eight o'clock this morning and she hadn't had the time yet to refresh her make-up, so what could you expect. They were all like that in Cosmetics & Perfumery, groomed to within an inch of their lives, glossy, glamorous girls who might as well be from another planet. Amy had always thought them a shade intimidating to the average woman who had just struggled in from the street, hair blown off course by the vicious air-con apparatus by the door. To be accosted at that moment by one of the Cosmetics team was not generally appreciated.

As well as the fast-fading make-up, Amy was also a little self-conscious today, showing off her new haircut. She could kill Amanda, never mind that she was one of the top stylists in the store's Hair & Beauty Salon up on the top deck.

What was it with hairdressers when you gave them the nod to trim? True, goaded by that scissor-happy stylist to go for it she had given the thumbs up for something new, fed up with the shoulder-length bob she had had for years but she had not envisaged such a drastic change. The elfin look took years off her and that was the last thing she wanted if she was to be taken seriously. Unable to stop herself, she ran her fingers through it, shocked at how short it felt before glancing pointedly at her watch. 'If that's all, Bea...?'

'Sure. Is he in?' she said, indicating the door to Daniel's office.

'No, sorry.' Amy had no idea where he was but then she seldom knew as he never bothered to inform her.

'Oh. Never mind, I'll catch him later. Bye.' Bea waved a French-manicured hand and went out leaving Janet, little, plump, homely Janet, to give Amy a truly sympathetic smile.

'You look exhausted, love.'

Janet, here since the year dot, called everyone 'love', male and female alike, although she became sweetly formal sometimes, insisting for instance on addressing Daniel as Mr Coleridge. Amy valued Janet's opinion. She thought of her as a mother figure although at close on sixty Janet was a couple of years older than her own. She could let her guard down with Janet and she needed her as back-up if Daniel had one of his occasional frustrated outbursts when sometimes his more creative ideas met with a stony response. Janet was very much a calming influence and, as with all senior secretaries, there was little that escaped her notice. In fact, Amy was of the opinion that if they took away the senior secretaries the place would fall apart.

'Do *you* know where he is?' Amy asked her, glancing towards the closed door.

'No. But he said he would be back by half four. He seems very relaxed today. I think he's quite optimistic that we'll reach our target.'

'I'm glad somebody is.' Amy smiled at her. Janet knew exactly what was what and the two of them had no secrets. She was under the impression that because Amy lived alone and was frantically busy she did not eat enough and occasionally she would produce a pie of some description as it was just as easy to make two as one. 'It's not over yet so we have to keep up the momentum,' she went on. 'I've been giving everybody the pep talk but the trouble is people are getting tired.'

'Don't I know it? I'm shattered by the time I get home.'

'Same here. We have to keep spirits up as much as we can. Mr Armitage is expecting a miracle and we don't want to disappoint him, do we?'

She hoped that remark did not come over as sarcastic because she knew Janet was fond of the man. Mr Armitage, the store manager, had a lot to answer for but the staff loved him and his easy-going smiley ways and so did she, and that was what made it so difficult. Any criticism of him was like telling a mother her baby was ugly. He abhorred change of any kind, which was why this store was stuck in a time warp. Cosmetics & Perfumery and Menswear on the ground floor had been revamped last year but things got progressively worse the higher up you went and the restaurant and toilets on the fifth were in serious need of a complete makeover.

'Do you want a coffee?'

'Have I time? I'm seeing Mr Armitage in twenty minutes.' Amy checked her watch. 'By the way, it's looking messy down on the second floor. There were things lying about. They should know by now that they must pick up and re-hang at once. We are high end, Janet, not bargain basement. I appreciate it's very busy down there but I don't want it to be like that when Mr Coleridge comes back. You know how eagle-eyed he is.'

'I'll give them a ring. Americano, no sugar?'

She nodded. 'It was frantic up in the restaurant. Not a spare seat anywhere. We've got to reorganize the seating arrangements when we do the refurbishment, somehow find the space to bring in more seating and tables. The last thing people want is to be standing there holding a tray with their food going cold and nowhere to park their bums. Where's the feel-good factor in that?'

'Don't tell me. It's the saving seats thing,' Janet reminded her. 'People still do it and it causes havoc.'

'I don't like the idea of issuing orders to customers but maybe we should put up a polite notice. No saving seats.'

'There's one up already but everybody ignores it. I suppose we could have somebody on hand to arrest them.' Janet's smile lit up her face. 'The fact is, Amy, love, we could run the whole thing so much better if we didn't open to the Great British Public.'

'My sentiments exactly. Janet, what would I do without you?' They laughed and thankfully some of the tension Amy was feeling evaporated. Only a few more days and the worst would be over.

'By the way ...' Janet lowered her voice. 'I hope you don't mind me saying but you've got a ladder in your tights.'

'Have I?' She checked it. Bugger. The tights were the barely black variety so it was very obvious. Worst of all, Bea, who never ever had a ladder in *her* tights would surely have noticed it.

They exchanged a small rueful smile.

Janet stood up to get the coffee, pausing to hand Amy a message.

'He's persistent, I'll give him that,' she said cheerfully. 'And he's a lovely man if you don't mind me saying. Believe me, good men are in short supply these days. Don't let him slip through your fingers. And another thing, I like the new hair. It takes years off you.'

'Does it? Do you really like it? I feel like Peter Pan, Janet.' Quickly Amy went into her cubby-hole of an office next door, blessedly finding a new pair of tights in her desk drawer and changing into them, wedged behind the door as she did so just in case Daniel barged through and caught her with her skirt hoiked up and what she considered to be her ample thighs on display.

After Janet brought the coffee through, she took a moment, gazing out onto the street as the daylight dwindled and lights came on and wondered what to do about Brian. Janet was quite right; at her age, unattached heterosexual males were thin on the ground.

She had no idea how it had happened, for she had never set out to get a boyfriend but then didn't they say that they came along when you least expected them? No, their eyes had not locked over the ready-meals cabinet at the supermarket but rather at an art exhibition when, as she puzzled over a particularly awful example, he had laughed in a kindly fashion and tried to explain what it was all about. For a moment she had thought he might be the artist himself, which would have been a terrible faux pas but luckily he was not, merely a guy looking to buy something. They ended up having a coffee together and that was very much that. Bea would consider Brian to be a hunk, too, if she ever set eyes on him but he was all hers and Bea was not getting a look in.

She found herself smiling. At their age, 'boyfriend' was not the right word. 'Gentleman friend' was ridiculous. They were not yet at the 'partner' stage and referring to him as her 'lover' sounded daft. They had been going out for the past three months and he had invited her to spend Christmas with him but that would mean cancelling with her mum and dad.

She was guilty, she knew, of leaving a change of plan much too late because her mother liked Christmas arrangements to be settled by November at the latest and after that they were written in stone.

Her parents did not know about Brian but it was stupid

trying to keep him a secret from them. She knew she blew hot and cold and that a less persistent man would have given up on her long since but she liked to have her life mapped out and she really did not have time for a man in that life, certainly not just now, and he had to understand that.

She had seen the women who tried to have it all, an exciting career, a husband and children.

It might work for them but it would not work for her.

The only truly successful women she knew and admired had chosen the path they wanted to take and that meant remaining single and focused so that the people who mattered took you seriously. Sometimes she wished she had never met Brian. Love at first sight was a fairy tale and she was far too practical a person to be swept off her feet. A mad attraction at first sight was another matter entirely. He was also rich and successful and although she knew it ought not to be, it proved to be a powerful aphrodisiac.

He had caught her at a low ebb, that was all, and she had made it plain that she was not interested in a long-term relationship so if *he* was, he could forget it. It had taken a lot of nerve to tell him that on their second outing and he had merely raised his eyebrows as if to say that that had never been his intention, either. She had also made a cock-up of asking him what his marital situation was within minutes of meeting him, embarrassing both of them, but she needed to know before she accepted a dinner invitation because the last thing she could cope with was a man with baggage attached.

'Not guilty,' he told her with a laugh. 'My God, you're good with the third degree, aren't you? Anything else you want to know before you let me off the hook?'

It had made her feel awkward because it sounded as if she was just using him for sex, which was quite a dreadful thing to admit to. On the contrary, he was an interesting man although cagey about how he earned his money, which made her ask him laughingly if it was legal. All she knew was that he traded online in art and antiques, which could mean anything. It was lucrative, though, judging by his lifestyle.

The truth was she had a challenging job and she had no time for diversions. She had a limited social life because she had moved away from home and all her old girlfriends and working as she did it was difficult to make new ones. Daniel thought she was all business and this place was a hot-bed for rumours; it would weaken his belief in her if he found out she was in the throes of an affair. If she were to take up with Brian it would certainly please Janet. She had been remarkably discreet since she had met the two of them together – an accidental out of work bumping into each other sort of meeting. Brian had been given her stamp of approval but then he was the sort of good-looking charmer whom the older ladies adored.

Amy wanted the relationship to continue a while because she had forgotten just how delightful it was to have a man tell her she was lovely, to buy her flowers, all that romantic nonsense. She was achingly aware, however, that there would have to be a moment, before it got way too serious, that she would pull the plug on it without upsetting him too much but in the meantime there was no harm in admitting to her parents that he actually existed.

Before she could help herself she picked up the phone and dialled his mobile.

She panicked a moment as she heard it ringing and then, as he picked up she momentarily lost the ability to speak.

'Is that you, Amy? Everything okay?'

'Yes,' she said, giving a little cough to disguise the tremble in her voice. What the hell was the matter with her? 'Look, I've been thinking. Why don't you come over to my parents for Christmas? They'll be delighted to meet you.'

Chapter Two

Snape House, Christine's home for close on thirty years, nestled in the Ribble Valley. It was at the edge of the village of Downill, a place of pretty stone-built cottages and a splendid church, the sort of typical English village beloved of television producers hoping to sell their offerings worldwide.

Before Christine and Frank discovered it they had been on the look-out for a suitable property for some time, something grand in a Victorian rectory type of way, big but not too big with a large but easy to manage garden and unspoilt views. It had to be within a reasonable commuting distance to Preston where the business was located but not too remote as Christine, mother to two small children, did not wish to be stranded completely.

It was a tricky brief for the estate agent and of course they knew they would never find the ideal place but as they scoured the county, dragging the children along with them, they began to despair.

It was Frank's dream to own a country house of character as befitted what he saw as his rising standing in the local business community. His father was a shy man and had never pushed himself forward but Frank was more than happy to do so, seeing networking as essential, although it had to be said that part of it was that he felt he had something to prove to Christine's father, who had never thought him up to much. Owning even a modest country house would be stretching their budget and she could have asked her own family for financial assistance but because they did not entirely approve of her marriage, she was in no mood to ask favours. In any case, Frank would rather stuff a bee in his mouth than ask for help and she much admired that streak of independence.

Frank had been fast-tracked into taking the family business on after his father's declining health forced his early retirement and Frank had relished the opportunity presented to him. He had visions of a bright future at the head of a booming business and so Christine was persuaded that a house move, onwards and upwards, at this moment in their lives would be to their advantage. If they did not grasp the opportunity now, he told her, they would start having second thoughts and would never do it.

Downill, lying in the picturesque Beacon Fell Country Park, had escaped their notice previously because it lay outside the circle they had drawn, adding a further half hour to Frank's commute. Fate can play a tricky hand sometimes, though, and perhaps if the sun had not been shining that day out of a cloudless blue sky, perhaps if the little gardens of the cottages on Bamber Lane had not been stocked full of summer flowers, perhaps if the people sitting at tables outside the Fox & Hounds enjoying lunch had not looked so happy and contented, it might have been a different story.

Crossing the little stone bridge that spanned the river it was like a fairy-tale village in the picture books she read to the children and she said as much to Frank, who was thinking figures putting him in a much more practical frame of mind. They were through the village within minutes but it was all too late, for she had already caught her first glimpse of the house with its splendid collection of chimneys; a mansion of pale-grey stone, of a neat symmetrical design with part of the frontage covered with Virginia creeper. Its garden with its wooded area, wide borders and vast lawns was far too big; it also bordered the river, which was dangerous for the children and the house itself had two or three bedrooms too many and the sheer size of it would make it a nightmare to maintain. However its dilapidated state and the fact that it had been empty and steadily getting worse over the last two years meant that it just about fitted into their price range.

But, even as Frank muttered something about 'too far out' as he manoeuvred the car up its winding drive past a bank of overgrown rhododendrons, even before she viewed the horrors of the interior, she knew that this was it. They would come in with a cheeky offer and who knows, it might just be accepted.

It was.

The defining moment for the Fletchers that Christmas had really begun was the switching-on of the fairy lights on the tree. Christine counted everything else, writing and sending the cards, buying and wrapping the presents and so on as pre-Christmas stuff. Now that the cards and the accompanying short note were in the post she worried that she had made Amy sound much too self-centred and wished now that she had not called Monique *darling* when she had not accorded that title to her own daughter. Sometimes she wondered why she bothered to put the note in with the cards but once you started these things it was difficult to stop. People expected it; the yearly Fletcher news bulletin.

She always went for the positive slant anyway to the extent of making light of Frank's illness, which at the time had been devastating and for a good while afterwards had been a grave concern. His father had died of a heart attack as had his grandfather so a quick popping-off unfortunately ran in the Fletcher family. She tried her best to keep him healthy but he did not exercise other than an occasional round of golf, which was more to do with keeping up contacts than actually enjoying the game.

*

The Saturday before Christmas was a dreary December day with the lights on from the word go. A low mist hung about by the river first thing, a mist suspended above the water as if it were a ghostly magical cloud; eerie, chill and beautiful, dispersing as the temperature rose above freezing. The last of the leaves lay in a crisp bedraggled heap in one forgotten corner of the garden and Christine yearned for snow, for at least then it would look pretty again. Downill in the snow was the stuff of nostalgic calendars. However, she did not want snow just yet because she needed Amy to get herself across the Pennines in one piece and that little car of hers was not built for winter driving on that infamous road over the moor.

She was so intent on putting the final touches to the tree that she did not notice Frank coming into the room. She was startled as, sensing a presence, she spun round to face him. He was in one of his miserable moods again, hovering, at a loss as to what to do when he was at home supposedly relaxing, but relaxing did not come easily to him. His was the sort of personality that ploughed relentlessly through life irrespective of whom or what he pushed aside in the process. She supposed they called it being focused, which seemed to be the buzz word these days. Despite the cheery mention on her Christmas note she dreaded his retirement for then they would be together all day long with no respite and her carefully managed routine would be severely disrupted.

He was a difficult man and she had known that when she married him but had made that age-old mistake of thinking she could change him. The not unexpected diagnosis of a potential heart problem earlier in the year had left him with a depression that lingered. She owed it to him to help all she could but the down moods were starting to affect her, too, and she could not allow that to happen. He was respected at work, she knew that, but was he liked? Shirley who ran the office adored him from afar, of course, and she used to tease him about that until he started to react badly so she wisely put a stop to it.

Their marriage was floundering, had been for years, but Christine had been brought up a Catholic. She was lapsed now, but the basics stuck with her, that constant guilt, and made the thought of divorce impossible. In any case, where on earth would she go if she left him? She had money of her own, could buy something else but she loved this house, her home, and she had no intention of giving it up. Leaving Frank, although briefly considered, was not an option. Who knows, things might get better; they had gone through difficult times before and here they were, still together.

'For heaven's sake, don't creep up on me like that,' she said, wobbling a little. 'Can't you see I'm standing on a stool? You nearly gave me a heart attack,' she added knowing at once that it was the wrong thing to say. 'Oh, sorry, darling.'

He managed a small smile. 'No danger of that. You'll outlive me.'

'Don't say things like that. That little op sorted you out, didn't it?'

Looking back, the health scare had been a good thing, a warning, which had brought him up sharply and been the incentive he needed to stop smoking and start eating more healthily. Sadly there was no way she could stop him fretting about the business, which had taken a bit of a downturn this past couple of years but then in this day and age everyone was surely in the same boat. They owned a removal company and the fact was very few people were moving at present. There were always people moving with their jobs and that would never change but it was the moving house just for the sake of it that had been stopped in its tracks.

'Nearly done.' Christine, still precariously balanced on the stool when there was a perfectly good set of sturdy steps in the back porch, reached across and looped a silver star over the tree top. 'There.'

She stepped off the stool and stood back.

'Can I help?' Frank asked belatedly regarding the finished tree with a frown. He was a heavily built man, lately edging towards plumpness, which they were trying desperately to control but he had kept his good head of hair of which he was proud and there wasn't a grey hair in sight. Christine had a few – and no wonder – but her regular trip to the hairdresser took care of that. She had opted to remain dark-haired shying away from the hairdresser's attempts to persuade her otherwise. Unadventurous, she wore it in the same style she had had for years; falling to shoulder length from a side parting, which meant it was versatile and she could if she wanted bunch it up off her face to show off her high cheekbones, an inherited feature that meant she would age well.

'What do you think?' She thought the tree looked gorgeous standing in the corner of the drawing room and, after all the hard work she was not in the mood for criticism.

'Do you want the truth?'

'Go on.' She gave him one of her looks.

'It looks a bit sparse. What's happened to the decorations? The stuff the kids made?'

'Oh come on, isn't it time we went for something a touch more elegant? I've still got them,' she added quickly. 'But I've left them up in the loft for now. Perhaps we'll get them out when we have grandchildren.'

'Sometime never then,' Frank said. 'You'll have to put that right out of your head. How many times do I have to tell you not to get your hopes up? Amy isn't into kids and I can't see Mike and Monique obliging any time soon.'

'I wouldn't be so sure about that.'

'I don't know what he sees in her, anyway,' he went on, determined, it seemed, to grumble.

'I wish you wouldn't talk about her like that.' Christine glanced anxiously round as if their daughter-in-law was standing outside the door.

'I'm only saying it to you, love. She needs to get herself a job for starters if she doesn't intend to have kids. What does she do all day?'

'She paints.'

'She paints,' he echoed mockingly. 'And that helps to pay the bills, does it?'

'You could help out. You could give Mike a rise, darling.' She tried a smile, hoping it might strike home. 'He works hard for you. He deserves it.'

'He does not. He still hasn't got the hang of it. He knows how to shift furniture, I'll give him that, but when it comes to the business side of things he's hopeless. He's supposed to do the marketing for Christ's sake. He's the one supposed to be getting our name out there.'

'Does he know that? You don't make it clear to him what he's supposed to be doing.'

'Don't tell me how to run the business. I tell you, Christine, if I dropped dead tomorrow that business would be up shit creek within months if he was in charge. Look what happened when I was off work.'

'We were all upset and Mike did very well keeping things on track.'

'With Shirley's help. Thank God for her. She could run it with one hand tied behind her back.'

She frowned, not wanting to be reminded of the office manager. No doubt Shirley, big brassy Shirley, thought she ran the show but the truth was she was not nearly as good as he thought and when Christine used to be in the office, admittedly in a part-time capacity, she had covered up a lot of Shirley's errors. Frank gave Mike no credit for how hard he worked and how he tried his best to please him and it annoyed her that he should dismiss Monique just like that, but then Frank didn't have a creative bone in his body so he could not understand how the creative mind worked.

'Mike needs a woman who will jiggle him along, somebody to push him instead of somebody who sits around all day doing bugger all except paint. I wouldn't care if they were any good.'

He was red-faced and she knew that getting upset was not good for him. With an effort she tried to calm him down. 'They're not that bad. They're quite nice in fact.'

'That's right. Defend her.' He hesitated. 'Did I tell you I spotted her a while back in a café in Lancaster talking to a bloke? They looked very cosy.'

'Not that again,' she said, annoyed that he wouldn't let it drop. 'I told you it was probably somebody she knew from school. She knows a lot of people here, Frank, so don't try to make it out to be something it wasn't, and for heaven's sake don't say anything to Mike about it.'

'Ah. So you do think there might be something in it?'

She exploded at that. 'Will you stop it? How many times do I have to tell you that she is *not* having an affair? She's as likely to have an affair as I am although having said that ...' she tried to lighten the mood and smiled. 'You're such a tosspot sometimes that nobody could blame me if I did.'

He managed a smile too. 'Sorry, love.' He rubbed his shoulders. 'God, they're like a board. I need a massage.' His smile widened. 'Any chance of that?'

Her thoughts were elsewhere. 'You never know, there might be an announcement over Christmas.'

'About what?'

'A baby,' she murmured, ever hopeful.

'They can't afford a baby. If I know you, you'd end up paying for the lot. Pram. Cot. Decorating the nursery. You name it, we'd be coughing up for it.'

'I wouldn't mind in the least. It will be our first grandchild, Frank, so we'll have to help out all we can.' She hesitated, deciding it was much too early to mention school fees and the plan she had for those. Her parents' unexpected deaths in a motorway pile-up had left her in a state of disbelief and shock but later there had been some small compensation when she realized that they would have wanted it like that, to die instantly together, and there was the added bonus of the money and property that came her way. She was the only child so she got it all and, as well as propping up their business – a decision not taken lightly – she invested a chunk of it, which was intended to be spent on the grandchildren's education, the grandchildren that had yet to appear. 'Mike and Monique might have to think of a bigger house when a baby comes along,' she added watching him closely as she allowed that little thought to sink in.

'Those two have had enough out of me already.' His frown deepened. 'Has she said something about a baby?'

'No but I wouldn't be at all surprised. She's been a little odd lately and it's time, isn't it? They've been married for five years and it's time.'

She knew she had to be patient. People started their families later these days. Mike was only thirty-four and more importantly Monique was not yet thirty so there were no worries yet about biological clock-ticking. It was such a relief that she and Monique got on so well and they often popped into each other's homes for a coffee and a chat. In fact although she did not care to admit it, she got on much better with her daughter-in-law than her own daughter.

'It's their decision whether or not they have a baby, not ours. You wouldn't have liked it if my mum had put pressure on us, would you?'

She had been pregnant straight off, the month following their wedding, so that argument did not carry any weight but she saw from Frank's tone that the subject was closed. He was right. It was none of her business and she had to stay out of it.

She moved the stool out of the way.

'All ready,' she said. 'Do you want to do the honours?'

They had had the fairy lights for years, lights that were bundled unceremoniously into the box and stuffed back in the attic year after year.

'Are we taking bets on whether they work or not this year? It'll be a miracle if they do.' He was poised over the switch, smiling.

'Just get on with it,' she urged, crossing her fingers as he started the daft countdown in a faux American accent as if he was in the control room at Cape Canaveral, after which the tree lights flickered immediately into life. They shared a smile at that and a warm feeling ignited in her, too. Like any other couple, they had their ups and downs but it wasn't all bad.

'Thank God for that. I told you we didn't need to buy new ones. It's a complete waste of money. Those will last us for years yet.'

'You tight so and so,' she said, laughing, though, as she said it. It was a relief to laugh because now, with the tree up, the fickle lights on, the cards despatched, the presents bought, she could concentrate on the final preparations for her guests.

'Sit down for a minute,' Frank said, showing uncharacteristic concern suddenly. 'You look like death.'

'Thanks for that,' she said tartly. 'That's just what a girl needs to hear.'

'You haven't stopped today. Does it always have to be such a panic?'

'I'm not panicking,' she told him. 'Everything's under control. I've just got a few last minute groceries to get on Monday and everything else is being delivered. It's all in hand.'

'There'll be far too much as usual. We'll be living on leftovers for a fortnight afterwards.'

'That's Christmas for you,' she said, determined to be cheerful. 'I wouldn't have it any other way although you'll have to watch what you eat this year. You've got to look after your blood pressure.'

'I'll have what I want and to hell with it. Pegging out

after a good dinner can't be such a bad way to go.'

'Don't joke.'

'Who says I'm joking?' He was sitting in the chair opposite, tapping agitated fingers on the arm. He had changed since the scare and not for the better; the terseness that had always been there under the surface suddenly much worse. It was understandable because he was stressed; worried because the illness had taken him by surprise although it shouldn't have, not with his family history. She was reminded of her mother's gloomy forecast when she had first introduced him into her family.

'Does he have moods?' her mother had asked, yet another nail in the coffin so far as she was concerned. 'You really have to watch a man with moods, darling. They can be tiresome.'

In love, in that blissful state, she was in no mood for any criticism of her man and in that age-old tradition her parents' opposition made her all the more resolved to marry him. Now she had to admit that her mother had been right and Frank's down moods were beginning to affect her too.

'It'll be a nice family Christmas,' he said, finally managing the smallest of smiles as if he could read her thoughts. 'Sorry if I've been a bit snappy lately but I'm worried about the business.'

'I know.' She sighed and wished there was something she could do to help him. 'Everything will be fine, you'll see.'

He nodded. 'I'm looking forward to a few days off. Just the two of us and the kids and we know Monique well enough by now not to be too concerned if the carrots burn.'

'I'm not worried about that. It's Amy....' She adjusted the cushions behind her back and sighed, remembering the last painful phone call. Amy was not good on the phone, always sounding as if she was looking at her watch, just about to go out somewhere terribly important with no time for a chat. 'I'm not even absolutely sure that she'll be here. She has a big presentation to prepare for early in the New

Year in Manchester and she sounded as if she was using that as an excuse for maybe not making it.'

'Don't be ridiculous.' For a moment he seemed in a genuine panic. 'Of course she will. She's never missed it yet. And what the hell would she do if she didn't come here? Spend it all alone in that miserable little flat eating a ready meal or beans on toast? You know she can't cook for toffee.'

'It's not a miserable little flat,' she said, remembering how nice she had made it sound in the Christmas note.

'It's not great, either. I told her I would pay the extra rent if she went for that bigger place but she wouldn't hear of it. But then, that's my girl,' he added proudly. 'Too bloody independent for her own good.'

'I wish she had some friends,' Christine continued, watching Frank closely. She knew the cause of some of the agitation; the no smoking and low-fat diet regime was hell for him. She suspected he was still smoking occasionally on the sly because she could smell it on him but she had yet to catch him in the act.

Amy was work-obsessed just like her father and it was no surprise that she was doing so well. She knew in her heart that their daughter would have made a much better job of taking over the family business than Mike, the son who was being groomed to do just that whether he liked it or not. 'Doomed to take over' might be a better description of his fate and she really ought not to have said in the Christmas note that he was enjoying shadowing his father when the opposite was the case. He had little interest in the business but, when he failed at school so spectacularly with any hopes of going to university down the pan, going into the family business had been the only option. Frank loved the job and had built things up considerably and being a local firm, Fletcher's Removals & Storage was often the first choice for people in the area. As for Mike, Christine suspected he was just sticking with it because he did not wish to disappoint his father and that, if he had a free choice, he would prefer to be somewhere else, doing his own thing, doing what *he* wanted. Sometimes she even wished he would show them what he was made of and simply tell his dad to stuff the job. It would serve Frank right, for he treated him abominably and expected far more of him than anybody else. For some reason he had always had a short fuse where Mike was concerned. She had been present once when he had given his son a right bollocking for a mistake that had, admittedly, cost them dear but it was a mistake anybody could have made and she had seen the look on Mike's face and had to fight back a desire to round on Frank there and then and tell him just what she thought of him for giving his son a dressing down in public.

But then she had never known her son lose his cool in his life. Mike was laid back, easy going, and, although she loved his choice of girl, she could not help feeling that Frank was right in a way and it might have been better for him if he had chosen somebody with a bit more fire in her belly. Monique was a sweet girl, childlike in many ways, and Mike adored her but she was of a dreamy nature and if she did have a child she would have to grow up quickly. She was also hopeless with money, poor darling, but that was a little secret between them and Christine was pleased she was able to help out. They went shopping regularly and she always bought Monique something from that little vintage shop she was fond of, as well as treating them to lunch, of course. Monique's parents were divorced, her father re-married and the mother's whereabouts were vague to say the least, which was so sad and made Christine even more determined to look after the girl. She had taken on the role of mother-substitute with a vengeance.

'Why doesn't Amy have friends, Frank?' she persisted, the thought troubling her greatly. 'She's pretty enough and successful but she never talks about any friends and we haven't seen any around when we've been over. I wish she'd find herself a nice man and settle down.'

'By that you mean you want her to get herself married and start a family – that's what settling down means to you. Don't bring that up at Christmas. We don't want an atmosphere like last year.'

'That wasn't my fault. There are so many subjects we can't mention. She can be touchy.'

'And so can you.'

She glanced at him, irritated because in his eyes his daughter could do no wrong. Never mind that she had let him down badly, never mind that she had destroyed his dreams of joining him in the family business; she was still his favourite child.

'She has to lead her own life, Christine,' he continued, quiet and earnest now. 'She's going places in her job and just because she's decided that marriage and kids is not for her you accuse her of being abnormal.'

'I didn't say that,' she said hotly. 'I never said that.'

'Just think before you speak and don't mention her lack of friends. It's no big deal. I don't have many friends, either.'

'But you're a man. It's different.'

'I'm not getting into that. Look....' he glanced at his watch. 'Would you mind if I popped into the office for an hour? I just have a few things to settle.'

'I thought things were tailing off,' she said, trying to hide her irritation, for she knew damned well what an hour meant. She also wondered if Shirley would still be there but she quickly put that thought out of her head. 'Who on earth wants to move house at Christmas?'

'You know as well as I do that people do. We have three moves on next week and one is a long trek so the lads will have to get the stuff down to Kent, stay over and unpack next day. It's going to take forever because it's a full unpacking set-up and I've told the lads they can play it by ear and put the Christmas tree up as well if they have time, even though, strictly speaking, it's outside our brief.'

'Off you go, then, but do be back in time for Amy.' She bit her lip, stopping herself from mentioning the smoking because it really was up to him. He knew the score as well as she did and nagging had never worked with Frank.

'Stop worrying. You have a rest while I'm out. You look tired out, sweetheart.' He came over and dropped a gentle kiss on the top of her head and just for a minute it was the old Frank and she remembered why she had married him. She was just twenty-one and far too young to get married, upsetting everybody in the process although, seeing she was beaten her mother had rallied round and the wedding itself had been the stuff of dreams with the cream of the Lancashire county set invited.

It sometimes occurred to her that, if her parents had been more supportive of Frank, had liked him a little more, that it might have tailed off but their very opposition, their desire for her to marry into another wealthy local family had made her all the more determined to marry him. Frank was new money if you were talking old values, a little rough round the edges and spoke with a Lancashire accent but it was the twentieth not the eighteenth century and that sort of thing should not matter anymore. How foolish, because it mattered every bit as much. In the event, her parents mellowed over the years, loving their grandchildren, spoiling them, growing to respect Frank in turn although she was sure they never liked him but it was a relief in a way that they were no longer around because she would have hated to admit to them that perhaps with that wonderful thing – hindsight – she *had* been a touch hasty.

After Frank was gone, she made herself a cup of coffee. The daylight or what had passed for it today was fading fast and although it was only mid-afternoon she switched on the lamps and drew the curtains over. They were not overlooked and they kept the whole house at a constant pleasantly warm temperature but it felt cosier to shut out the late afternoon gloom. She loved this room, the formal drawing room that had been off-limits to the children when they were young. This was the grown-up room with its silky striped sofas and beautiful pieces of antique furniture that she had lovingly collected over the years.

Sipping her coffee, Christine sighed, catching sight of the family photographs on a side table. There was one of her parents and Frank's parents, of Amy at sixteen, dark hair up in a ponytail, eyes shining, looking so pretty and one of Mike, a year younger, already struggling with his school work whereas his sister just sailed through.

If only Monique would have a baby, then she could take on the role of grandmother with enthusiasm but she could hardly suggest it outright – although she had given more than enough hints. Frank was right yet again for she knew she was wasting her time with Amy. She was tempted to ring her right now but it was a work day for her and you never knew what important meeting she might be in. She rarely rang her at work, although that Janet woman sounded very nice and always put her through if possible.

She would ring Monique instead, knowing that her beautiful, shy daughter-in-law would be much more agreeable to dropping whatever she might be doing for a girly chat. In the event the phone line was busy and she did not bother to leave a message. She would try later.

Chapter Three

Monique Fletcher was on the phone to her lover Sol.

'Hello darling,' he said at once, when she picked up even before she recited the number.

'How did you know it was me?' she asked irritably. 'I could have been anyone.'

'There's never anybody else there. You are neurotic these days.'

'I wish you wouldn't ring me at home on this phone,' she persisted. 'To be honest I'd rather you didn't ring at all but if you do, use my mobile.'

'You are joking? How could we have an intimate conversation if you're in the middle of Tesco?'

'Text me, then.'

'Like hell. Texts can be traced, darling.'

'And so can phone calls,' she replied tartly.

'What's your problem? Is he having you watched? Is the phone bugged?' His voice was full of derision and she very nearly slammed the phone down on him. Solomon Diamond – yes that really was his name – could be rude and arrogant, qualities she abhorred, but on the flip side there was this sexy languorous man that she found unbelievably exciting and attractive. One touch from him and she took leave of all her senses and she hated that she was so in thrall to him. 'What's your problem, Monique?' he repeated. 'It's the middle of the afternoon. That husband of yours is at work, isn't he?'

He never referred to Mike by name, always a variation of 'that husband of yours'.

'He is but that's not the point. He could have answered the phone and then what would you have said?'

His laugh was low, untroubled. 'Wrong number or I could have pretended I was calling about double glazing and he would have put the phone down pretty damned quick. What happened last week? I was all ready for you, my darling. I even ironed the sheets because I know how pernickety you are.'

She smiled a little at that word but he was not getting round her as easily as that. 'It's all very well for you but it's not easy for me to get away.' She perched on the chair beside the little table where the phone sat. On the table there was a vase filled with her favourite cream roses. Mike had come home with them the other day. It wasn't even her birthday but then he was so thoughtful on occasion. She touched one of the petals, dipped her head so that the scent drifted up, feeling suddenly a little sick. This deception was beginning to eat away at her. She was playing a dangerous game and she had to stop. 'I told you at the start that you mustn't expect too much of me,' she said speaking softly although she was quite alone. 'Christine always wants to know where I am and what I've been doing. I'm worried that she's going to get suspicious if I keep sneaking off to Lancaster for hours on end.'

'Why should she? You must learn how to lie. It's a useful trait, Monique. The alternative is to pack all this in, leave that fuckwit of a husband of yours and come and live with me.'

'Don't be ridiculous,' she said knowing that he would run a mile if she took him up on that. Sol was a loner and liked the single life. She knew she was taking a huge risk. She also knew that he could turn nasty and start to blackmail her any time he liked but she did not think that would happen. Sol was too lazy and too unconcerned about money to be a blackmailer. She had known him for a long time, long before she met Mike, but it was a chance encounter a few months ago that set it all off again. He had been living down in London for years but had grown tired of city life and come home. Meeting up with him unexpectedly, she was pleased to see him again. They were both grown-ups so there seemed no harm in going for a coffee with him to have a chat about old times but she had never meant it to escalate, never meant to accept his invitation to pop round to his flat, never meant for things to take off from where they had been left all those years ago. Walking round to his flat that day she had known what was going to happen by the look in his eyes and had felt faint with anticipation. In the event, they never made it as far as the bed that day. It was exciting and dangerous and stupid and she was risking a lot just for a few hours with him, at his flat, in his bed. It was also unbelievably sordid and that was exactly why she had made the decision to put a stop to it. She had tried to end it before but it had not worked. She was weak where Sol was concerned; she had to find strength from somewhere to put an end to it once and for all.

'Where *are* you?' she asked wondering if he was at his shop, if there was anyone listening in as she rewound the conversation in her head. It would be just like him to do something like that, to want to shock anybody who might be browsing amongst his bookshelves. If so, it was asking for trouble because he only had to mention her name and that would be a potential giveaway for there were very few women named Monique around here. 'Are you at the shop?' she went on, her alarm making her voice raise a notch.

'No, of course not, I'm at home. I've closed early. It's been dead all week and Rose wanted to do some shopping so I let her go.'

Rose was the middle-aged lady who helped him out. Rose was an astute woman and that was why Monique was careful never to set foot in the shop in case the sexual electricity that sizzled between her and Sol somehow showed on Rose's radar. It was unlikely that Rose would know Christine but there was no point in taking undue risks.

'Will I see you before Christmas?' his voice was low and confident for he knew damned well the effect he had on her. 'Here I am all alone about to spend Christmas in solitary confinement with nothing to do except watch crappy programmes on television.'

'I can't help that and there's no way I can escape the family,' she said, twisting the flex of the phone and wondering how to tell him what she knew she must tell him. 'Look, Sol, I've been doing a lot of thinking lately and—'

He laughed. 'Don't bother. You're about to tell me yet again that all this deception is killing you, that you love your husband and that you don't want to see me anymore.'

There was a moment's silence.

'Well, yes and please listen to me. It's been a mistake, Sol. I'm a married woman,' she said, the words comically prim, looking at her reflection in the mirror and pushing at her long silky fair hair. 'I have to be sensible.'

'Why, for fuck's sake?' His exasperation rose. 'We are discreet. Nobody need ever know. If you won't leave him then we can just carry on as we are for years. You need me, darling, so don't even think of ending it.'

The threat was there, unsaid.

She waited for him to plead with her, to tell her he loved her, words he had never used, not ever. She had never used them either, not to him. She used them to Mike but that was because it was expected of her. Mike was not overly demonstrative, rarely said the words but whenever he did he meant them and she always dutifully replied that she loved him too, which she supposed she did if love could be defined as feeling an affectionate fondness.

It was just sex for Sol, she told herself, as she replaced the receiver.

Looking at her bright eyes in the mirror, her flushed face, she knew that it was the same for her, that and the danger of playing with fire.

On her part there was one added ingredient, though.

There were no doubts where Sol was concerned.

She loved *him*.

Number Eight, River Terrace was a small cottage bang in the middle of the row, a narrow riverside path and a steep bank separating it from the river itself. It was little more than a fat brook at this point but when the rains came the water thundered down, although thankfully never in enough quantity to reach and spill over the top of the bank.

It was Monique's first proper home that she could call her own, bought with the help of a hefty deposit gifted by Mike's parents. Mike had been reluctant to accept financial help but she persuaded him that they must not allow silly misplaced pride to get in the way of taking the sensible course.

She did not tell him that Christine had also privately given her a substantial sum to help with the initial furnishing and that even now, years on, she could be relied on to hand over little helpful monetary gifts from time to time. Christine was from a family of means and in fact, as she told Monique, her marriage to Frank had been seen by her parents as a most definite downgrading of her social position. Her family tree was sound – Lancashire aristocracy no less – and when her parents died, blessedly instantly and together in a car crash, Christine copped the lot and an impressive lot it was and it was she who was propping up the business now that they were going through a lean spell.

Monique needed Christine's help because she earned very little from her paintings and Mike was paid a paltry sum by his father for the privilege of being humiliated at every turn. She suspected that the workforce laughed at him, the boss's son who was plainly useless. It was no wonder that Frank had no thoughts of retiring for it would go bottoms-up if it was left in Mike's hands. At least that was what her dear father-in-law thought. Of all of them she sometimes thought that Frank could see right through her to the core of her being, not taken in as the others were by the shy sweetness she chose to portray.

The truth was she had been a wild child although she kept that quiet because she knew Christine would not approve. Christine was quaintly old fashioned and she imagined that her mother-in-law thought of her as a one-man woman just because Christine had probably never slept with anybody other than Frank.

If only she knew. It was with some amusement that Monique could not actually recall the exact number of men she had slept with.

Monique quickly learned that you had to use the assets you were blessed with and she knew from an early age that she was the pretty one, the child people fussed over, and later she realized that attracting a man was easy. Men were becoming tired and bored these days with the glut of hard-faced ambitious competitive women. On the contrary, they loved vulnerability and she knew exactly how to play that part.

All her life her parents had largely ignored her, her father never quite forgiving her for not being the son he craved and her beautiful mother irritated by her because it meant the curtailing of some of her amorous activities. The marriage had been a sham and the divorce when it came was no surprise. Following the divorce, her parents both moved from Lancaster going their separate ways and, at eighteen, neither of them was keen on making a home for Monique so when she went off to art college, that was very much it. She was on her own. She had known Sol from the sixth form at school and they chose the same course at college, supposedly by pure coincidence.

She decided early on that a life of poverty, making ends meet, was not for her and although she knew the chances of meeting and snaring a millionaire were slim she was willing to settle for a comfortable existence. She and Sol became an item at college but she ditched him when she realized he was totally without ambition and would never amount to anything.

It was much more than a brief fling. He had meant a great deal to her and breaking it off with him had been one of the hardest things she had ever done. There might have been a child from that liaison but disaster was averted when she lost it naturally at nine weeks. She never told Sol for it was nothing to do with him but she was right to ditch him for her instincts were spot on. Sol, after a brief spell teaching art at some inner-city comprehensive down south, was now content to bum along. He lived now in a flat down by the canal in Lancaster in an area largely frequented by students so that nobody really knew anybody else and she could pop in and out of the flat without question.

Sol had been injured in an accident a couple of years previously, injuries from which he had recovered but the compensation had been immense and he now lived off that and the small income he managed from buying and selling second-hand books in the little shop he ran.

After college, Monique returned to Lancaster because she needed the familiarity of it and she had no wish to beg either of her parents to take her in. She took a lowly paid job and together with a girlfriend managed to rent a little flat in town. All she wanted out of life was a nice home, her own car and sufficient money to go shopping without counting every single penny because that really was a bore. At that point she decided to go for the marrying-a-man-with-money option.

For a time she had to face the prospect of going for an

older man but then as luck would have it Mike came along. She sussed out his background before the second date, liked the fact that he dressed well, wore good shoes, drove a new car and had an affluent air about him. Without actually checking out his bank balance she recognized him for what he was, the only son, a little spoilt, maybe, not particularly bright but that did not worry her unduly for she was bright enough for both of them.

As soon as she saw the family home, Snape House, she was suitably impressed knowing that few people could afford the upkeep of a house like that and, if she married into the Fletcher family, she saw she would be cushioned and cosseted and protected and what on earth was wrong with that.

In the absence of a good-looking millionaire, Michael Fletcher would do very nicely. He was of the right age, reasonably good looking and most important of all he absolutely adored her. Of course she could be a homemaker, he assured her earnestly, saying how refreshing that was in this day and age and there was nothing he would like better and he wanted a woman who was happy to stay home and look after the children when they came along.

She could live with that. Love, at least on her side, was not necessarily part of the equation. She liked Mike and that was enough. She accepted that he was laid back, had a genial nature, hated to upset people, but now he needed to be more assertive and his painful slowness in learning how to do that was beginning to upset her. She despised Frank and the way he treated his son; even Christine seemed unaware of what went on in the office. The business was going nowhere fast because Frank was such a tyrant and the workforce generally disliked him every bit as much as she did. She knew the feeling was mutual, that Frank did not like her, that he thought her paintings crap, that if he had her way she would be out there seeking a proper job.

A proper job was the last thing she wanted. She did not

want to be bothered with that for she loved the freedom of working from home, getting up around ten o'clock in the morning long after Mike had left for work, having a leisurely bath, making coffee and eating cereal and scrambled eggs whilst reading the morning paper from cover to cover. She would then get dressed and, if she felt like it, she might do some painting or now and again she might meet up with Sol for a naughty romantic liaison.

On several days a week, she drove her little car – a luxury Christine had helped her buy – the ridiculously short drive to Snape House for afternoon tea and if the weather permitted a stroll arm in arm with her mother-in-law round the gardens. Later, she would prepare dinner for when Mike arrived home, which could be as late as seven o'clock. He often needed soothing because he was frustrated by his father's refusal to listen to any of the ideas he might come up with to improve the business. If Frank had not thought of it himself then it was a no-no. She had never met a man who was so intransigent or as Mike said, bloody minded.

A couple of times a month she and Christine would take a trip into Preston and do some shopping. She would steer Christine to her favourite little boutique where Christine could be relied on to buy her a little something. Her wardrobe was heaving with the sort of vintage clothes she loved, not to mention the shoes and handbags, and sometimes if she had nothing else to do in the afternoon she would spend it trying clothes on, admiring herself and parading in front of the free-standing mirror.

She loved her little home although she was not quite so much in thrall with the village itself and she sometimes yearned for the bustle of a city existence but it was just too impractical a course to pursue, for their reliance on Frank and Christine was considerable. If Mike gave in his notice they could not be sure that his father would provide him with a decent reference and even if he did it would be looked on with suspicion and the truth was she could not risk losing Christine's support. She had thought once upon a time of trying for a diploma in education so that she could teach art but it was a fleeting notion because her heart was never in it and it would have meant getting up stupidly early and doing a full day at college and actually working for once.

In any case, she did not care for kids and although she pretended to Christine that a baby was on the cards one day it most certainly was not. Mike thought she was off the pill now, thought they had been trying for a while but each month she had to disappoint him and shake her head sadly. He was muttering now about seeing the doctor just to check all was well but she could put that off for a couple of years because of her age. Relax, she told him, and it will happen one day.

With Mike not minding very much how she furnished their home she had happily done exactly what she wanted and although it looked much the same on the exterior as the others in the row, inside it was quite a different matter.

The little living room that you stepped into directly from the street was aglow with rosy reds and deep pinks, sumptuous silky materials and fringed lacy throws covering the two comfortable sofas, which together with a leather armchair made up the seating arrangements.

'Bloody hell, Monique, it's like a tart's boudoir,' her dear father-in-law had said with a laugh when he first stepped through the door.

She took that on the chin although the remark hurt her. What did he know about interior design? He was happy to leave all that to Christine and although the thought had crossed her mind that she had not quite achieved the look she was after, that it was all slightly over the top, it was impossible to change a thing once that remark was uttered. She was not going to allow him to think that he could influence her in any way.

There was no television; she felt strongly that it would

have dominated such a small room although it of all things surprised people for how on earth could they exist without it? Quite well, thank you. They had an extensive collection of books as well as a selection of CDs so they never felt any desperate need to sit in front of a television screen. It was largely her decision and there were times when Mike wavered when he heard people at work discussing what they had seen on the box the night before but she always talked him round.

Frank thought they were bonkers but then he didn't have much of an opinion of his son and everybody knew that he would have much preferred to train Amy up as his second in command. Frank was proud of the business but, honestly, the way he talked it up you would think he ran a huge international organization at times instead of a small-time removal and storage concern. If Amy had gone into it she would have commanded the respect of the workers for she had that air of authority about her that was patently lacking in Mike. Amy was the golden girl even though she had upped and left them in the lurch deciding that working for her father was never going to work and going out into the bigger world instead.

'She broke her father's heart,' Christine had said once, in a confiding mood over coffee. 'He doesn't let it show, of course, but he always thought she would take over when he was gone. Everything was ready for her and then she just came right out with it one day that she was going into retail management. You should have seen Frank's face, Monique. I am trying so hard but I can never quite forgive her for doing that to him.'

'You poor thing.' Monique had given her a quick cuddle and hardened her own heart to Amy, blithely skirting over the issue of her relationship with her own mother that had never amounted to much, either. Whenever she and Amy met they were courteous to each other but it was all superficial for she knew that Amy resented her, too. Amy was a workaholic, scarily ambitious, but that was her misfortune.

'You've landed nicely on your feet, Monique.'

Monique recalled those words, deep with meaning, and it could have led to a full-blown row, for she had seen the danger signs in Amy's eyes knowing that she had a quick temper but she had turned the tables on her by saying sweetly that Amy must learn to relax a little more and find the time to smell the roses.

'Some of us need to work to earn money, Monique. We don't all have a man willing to look after us.'

'Poor darling. I do understand.' She had given her a winning smile knowing that the best way to wind Amy up was not to take up the bait.

'Not that I would ever want to be in the position of having a man take care of me,' Amy had finished stoutly but again Monique refused to take up the challenge, which infuriated her all the more.

She used the smaller of the two bedrooms upstairs as a studio. On the Sunday before Christmas, Monique, her pale blonde hair caught back in childish bunches tied with narrow black ribbons, was working in it, putting the finishing touches to a painting. Mike was out on a secret mission – probably a last-ditch attempt to buy her Christmas present.

She was trying a more commercial approach these days and concentrating on what she could sell; namely pretty watercolours of local scenes. She had handed some over to a shop in Lancaster that specialized in local craftware and they had seemed pleased with them so she was hopeful that they might display them prominently and maybe they would catch somebody's eye. She had also put some into a small exhibition organized for local artists and by pitching the price right had managed to sell several. Sol had offered to put some on display in his shop but she had declined that dubious offer.

Carefully, she added her name in the bottom right-hand corner.

Despite her supposed lack of ambition, her desire for an easygoing lifestyle, her lack of real success was beginning to get to her. She still just about held onto the belief that one day people might clamour to own one of her paintings. On the other hand, it was more likely that Frank Fletcher would crack a proper smile. She had known when she took up the course at art college that the chances of success out there in the real world were slim but she had hoped that eventually she might earn enough from her paintings to think of it as a proper career. Still, as Christine said she was young yet and there was lots of time so she must stay positive.

Leaning back and squinting at the canvas, she nodded at last with satisfaction. It was a painting of Beacon Fell. Christine knew quite a bit about local history and had told her that it got its name because in medieval times it was the ideal place to put up a string of lit beacons to warn of danger or to celebrate major events. From the high point there were panoramic views in all directions over Snowdonia and North Wales, the coast of Fylde, the Lake District and even on a clear day the Isle of Man. The air up there was forever clean and crisp and chill.

This painting was one of a series and she had sketched this one back last year, remembering the smell of summer as she spent a day up there, soaking up the atmosphere and taking a picnic with her. Christine offered to come along but she wanted to be alone because she could not paint and listen to Christine chattering at the same time.

'Do be careful up there on your own. It's a lonely place,' Christine had said. 'Take your mobile with you.'

'Of course,' she said knowing that she would leave it at home. She needed solitude away from a constant stream of trivial text messages and anyway, it probably wouldn't work up there. As it turned out she had a lovely day and never once did she feel worried about being alone. Up in her studio, recalling the scene vividly, she blew gently on the name she had just written on the painting. She used her maiden name professionally and it was unwise to change it.

Monique Fox.

She was born in France to a French mother and English father although they had moved to the northwest of England when she was just a few months old. It was so annoying that her parents had not persisted with teaching her to be bi-lingual, her mother deciding that if she was to be married to an Englishman and live in England then she would more or less abandon her own language. Once she started to dream in English her mother said then that was the time to give in. So, Monique could speak French no better or worse than any other student in this country.

There was a Christmas card – a large, expensive one with a Victorian snow-scene – from her father and his second wife. Her father now lived in Kent and she had not seen him for some considerable time. The card was not even written by him but was signed 'With best wishes from Trevor & Jill Fox', so obviously Jill had taken charge of the business of writing the cards. 'From Dad and Jill' would have been more appropriate and she wondered if it was a deliberate slight on Jill's part, who had never forgiven her for refusing to attend their wedding.

The letter from her aunt, her mother's sister, informing her of her mother's death had arrived last month and she had not discussed that with anybody other than Mike. She had been tempted to tell Christine and, in fact, invented an excuse for disappearing for a couple of days when, alone, she attended the funeral down in Sussex. She did not want the bucket-loads of sympathy Christine would offer and Mike understood that. She and her mother Isabelle had been estranged for years and so she could not bring herself to feel very much. Her Aunt Sylvie was there but even her relationship with her sister had been on cool terms and so it had been a dry-eyed affair at the local crematorium, the conveyor-belt effect painfully and rather amusingly obvious and afterwards the two of them, the sole mourners, had a meal in the hotel. Sylvie spoke English very well so at least that made things easier. Monique did not know her aunt at all and whenever her mother spoke of her it was with a sneer in her voice, 'posh tart' being the kindest thing she ever said about her.

'Does Trevor know?' Sylvie asked. Her aunt was very like her mother and as there was only a year's difference in age they might well have been twins. It was disconcerting to say the least although Sylvie had a softer look to her face and that subtle elegance of the Parisian lady.

'I think he must,' Monique said. 'I left a message on the machine.'

'You left a message?' Sylvie smiled thinly. 'If he had a shred of decency he would have turned up today for your sake if nothing else. It was the least he could do although I don't suppose he would have wanted that woman of his to be here. I certainly would not.'

'It wasn't Jill's fault.' Monique felt she ought to try to explain. 'It was over long before then so I don't suppose we can blame him for finding somebody else.'

'And where is your husband?' Sylvie said, immaculate in black, a pillar box hat completing her outfit. Like Monique, she was a tiny blonde lady although unlike her niece she chose to wear very high, spiky-heeled shoes.

'I didn't want Mike here today.' Monique twisted the rings on her finger.

'Why ever not? You need a husband's support at a time like this. He should have insisted on being here.'

'Mike's not like that.'

'Isn't he? Oh dear.' Sylvie glanced at her own hands, a large diamond and sapphire ring sparkling as it caught a sunbeam. 'Are you happy living up there?'

She talked as if Monique had a house on the moon.

'I have a lovely home. My husband and his mother are kind to me. I admit I don't like my father-in-law or my sister-in-law but that can't be helped.'

'You haven't answered my question. Are you happy?'

'I suppose I am.'

'You *suppose*? You made a mistake in marrying him.' It was a statement from a woman who knew what she was talking about. 'You married for clever reasons, I grant you that, because a little financial security is essential to life's happiness but you chose badly. I married for the wrong reasons, too, my dear, and I am not ashamed to admit that but at least I came out of both my marriages with a little pot of gold. If you left your husband where is *your* pot of gold? He is not rich enough. If you are going to go down that route then you must do it with flair. A man of modest means is simply not worth the bother.'

'I love Mike,' she protested, surprised that Sylvie could read her so well.

'You love yourself more, my angel. Like me, you are selfish and like me, your heart belongs to France. You should have married a Frenchman. They know how to treat a woman.'

'Really?' It seemed an odd thing to say coming from a woman who had married and divorced two of them.

'The English are cold. They have no passion in their souls. Look, Monique, I am at the end of the telephone if you need to discuss things. Why don't you come to stay with me for a while?'

'In Paris?'

She smiled briefly. 'That's where I live and you needn't make it sound such an unpleasant idea. We must stay in touch anyway so that we can sort out the finances and so on. You are aware of the terms of your mother's will?'

'Only that she left it all to you. Any money she had and the house she had here and the one in France. What is there to sort out?'

Sylvie shrugged, one of those wonderful Gallic shrugs. 'Did you ever see the cottage in Normandy?'

'No. I knew she inherited it years ago but I don't think she ever stayed there. Did she?'

'Once or twice. And I've been there too. But your mother was not interested in property and so I've been taking care of it for the last few years. A local couple look after it for me. Here.' she rummaged in her handbag. 'This is a photograph.'

Monique glanced briefly at it, not really interested. 'It looks lovely,' she said grudgingly, attempting to hand it back.

'No, keep it.' She sighed. 'I feel very cross with Isabelle. There was no reason to cut you out of her will. She should have left you something. She was such a vindictive woman and I have no idea why. What was your quarrel about?'

It was Monique's turn to shrug. 'I can't remember. I know she was opposed to my marriage even though she never met Mike and she thought I was stubborn just like my father.'

'That's no reason to disown you. What was she thinking of? Perhaps her mind was a little unbalanced. She was always far too sensitive a creature.'

'We shall never know,' Monique said flatly, for it was true. There was no point in having regrets and she was not going to twist herself into becoming a bitter woman by trying to unravel the reasons why her mother had disowned her. She had to live with the fact that she was born late in life to a couple who wished they had never had a child and that was one of the reasons why she had decided long ago that she was never going to inflict that emotional neglect on a child of her own. She thought fleetingly of the child she might have had. What a blessing losing it had been. 'Nevertheless I feel badly about it.' Sylvie sighed and patted her hand.

'Don't.' For once she was unconcerned about the money.

She didn't feel very much emotion, was incapable of that where her late mother was concerned.

'I mean it, Monique. You are most welcome to come and stay with me.'

'I can't leave Mike for any length of time.'

'Why not? It will do him good, make him appreciate you that bit more. Believe me, a little time spent apart from him will be time well spent and you might get somewhere with your paintings in Paris. It's always been the place to be for the budding artist and I have connections, my dear. You would, however, have to stop painting those dreadful bleak scenes of yours.'

'They sell.' Monique smiled a little. 'But I know what you mean. I want to get back to portrait painting. I think I have a talent for that.'

'You could paint me. How wonderful. I would love to have my lovely niece stay with me for a while. I've never had a daughter of my own, you see, so you are the next best thing.'

For a fleeting moment a shadow passed over her face and Monique saw that, underneath the glossy exterior, lurked a lonely middle-aged woman. It begged the question, though, of why women, particularly older ones, always wanted to mother her when her own mother had never cared a fig?

'Take care, my dear,' Sylvie had said, embracing her as they parted. 'And take my advice. Life, as we can see, is short and you owe it to yourself to be happy. So if all else fails, take a lover. It will spice things up. Believe me it can only be good for your marriage as long as your husband does not find out. That was the mistake I made. Henri was stupidly jealous although it was rather divine having two men fight over me.' She laughed but a rueful grimace accompanied it.

'A lover?' Monique felt her heart thud, knew her cheeks were blazing, knew also with a jolt that Sylvie was aware she had already found one.

So much for keeping a secret.

Chapter Four

For Christmas Daniel had bought them each a bottle of the newest, hottest perfume 'Bella-Sophia'. It was extravagant to say the least, particularly as she and Janet had agonized about whether or not it would be appropriate to buy him anything at all before settling for a joint present; a silk tie, chosen with the help of Marcus in Menswear. They despaired of Mr Coleridge in that department for he chose not to take up the offer of help with his attire insisting on going his own sweet way and in their opinion letting the side down big time. They were men of smart suits in that department and Mr Coleridge's ubiquitous jeans teamed with a casual jacket and open-necked shirt did not cut the mustard.

The handing over of gifts in the office had been a touch awkward, his little speech unexpected but sweet for all that.

'This is just a small thank you to you ladies for all you've had to put up with these last few months,' he said, reaching for the gifts, which they instantly saw had been professionally wrapped. 'I hope you like this. It had better be good because it's cripplingly expensive,' he went on, saying the wrong thing, his nervousness odd but strangely endearing. 'But Beatrice Galloway recommended it and what she doesn't know about perfume isn't worth knowing.'

Beatrice?

She and Janet exchanged a knowing glance.

Brian was not a good front-seat passenger but then she

knew few men who were. With the seat pushed back as far as it would go, he stretched out his long legs in a vain attempt to look as if he was relaxed. He had complained already about the size of the car, the colour – yellow – the bumpy ride, the lack of acceleration and just generally been Mr Grump. Finally his 'Are you sure we're going the right way?' had really got up her nose because she had done this particular journey so many times that the car very nearly knew the way itself.

'It's Christmas. Lighten up,' she told him, perversely almost wishing now that she had taken him up on his offer to use his much bigger and far more luxurious vehicle but *she* had invited *him* and it seemed important that she should provide the transport.

Despite his annoying sharp intakes of breath whenever she overtook, she accomplished the task of getting them there without mishap. It was a long drive and she intended to use it as an opportunity to chat; it was time she knew more about him. All the passion and lovey-dovey stuff was all very well but it did not give you much chance to actually talk as a couple and to dig a little deeper into his background. Having things in common was important, like it or not, and just now she was struggling to find anything that they might share or do together aside from the obvious.

The pre-holiday traffic was predictably busy, though, and it took all her concentration to drive safely so their conversation on this trip was of a general nature and she found out nothing more about his childhood, his earlier life or the women he had maybe loved and lost. He was older than her so there must be an interesting back story but other than saying he used to live in the southeast he was giving nothing away.

She was curious, not excessively so, but she had talked a lot at the beginning and given away a fair number of her own worries and concerns and perhaps with hindsight she had been a little indiscreet about her work. She saw what they meant by pillow talk because it was so tempting to talk about things to the man in your life, things that ought to be kept quiet. He was a good listener and it beat talking to herself, which, being on her own in her flat, happened a lot.

She wanted Brian to open up a little so that she knew more about what made him tick because his unwillingness to talk about his life was beginning to make her think that all was not as it appeared. In the meantime, she thought it necessary to warn him that, even though they were just friends, her parents might think they were serious about each other.

'Thanks for coming,' she told him once they were on a quieter road. 'They are looking forward to meeting you.'

'Me too. Christmas is all about families,' he said.

She did not take her eyes off the road but she detected in his voice a strange wistfulness and waited a moment for him to elaborate but he did not.

'My dad will want to know all about your prospects,' she went on, keeping cheerful. 'I hope you don't mind but he thinks I'm still about sixteen. Just humour him, will you?' She laughed at his muttered grumble. 'I hope you've brought your tax return form. He might want to check it.'

Her attempt at humour was lost on him. 'I have no intention of spoiling things by talking about work,' he said stiffly.

'It wouldn't spoil things for me. I am willing to do anything to stop them from bringing out the family photographs. Incidentally ... ' this time she stole the quickest of glances at him, 'where are yours? You don't have any at your place.'

'Any what?'

She stopped a sigh. Was he being deliberately obtuse? 'Family photographs,' she said. 'There are no photographs anywhere in your house.'

'So? Is that a problem?' He sounded irritated and that irritated her in turn. This relationship was all about highs and lows with no middle ground. Honestly, it was patently obvious that it was going nowhere if, three months in, they were already on the edge of serious bickering. 'I've told you, I don't have any family and that's the end of it. Just leave it. I don't want to talk about it.'

She waited for him to say more, to mellow his tone at least, in short to bloody apologize, but he did not and even though she could feel her own anger rising, now was not the time for an argument as they were at last on the narrow road leading to Downill which was all twists and turns, ups and downs and she needed all her concentration as the weather had turned nasty and the rain that had accompanied them for most of the journey was turning to sleet as they climbed. Visibility was poor now and she was conscious that a lot of accidents occurred near home when you were starting to relax and beginning to think of the end of the journey at last, looking forward to welcoming warmth and a cup of tea. She took the decision to slow down as she felt her car's grip on the road lessen and the tyres began to throw up slush and on cue, Brian urged her to be careful as there was a lot of standing water on the side of the road.

'Who's driving this car?' she said tetchily. 'Me or you?'

And at that he subsided into miffed silence.

'You didn't tell me it was quite so grand,' Brian broke what had started to be an uncomfortable silence as she swung the car through the gates. She decided magnanimously to forgive him as sulking was not the best way to start the Christmas break and her mother would notice at once if the atmosphere between them seemed strained.

'It's not that grand.' But she supposed through his eyes it might be. It was only a small-scale country house but the gardens were impressive and in summer were truly spectacular.

She drew the car to a halt on the gravel, pulled on the handbrake and sighed, in no immediate hurry to get out.

She needed to take a moment before she faced her mother and the inquisition that would follow.

'How many staff do they employ?' Brian clicked open his seatbelt and turned a little to face her.

'Just two,' she said defensively. 'A gardener and Jean who helps Mum in the house a couple of mornings a week.'

'I see. What does your mother do again?'

'She's good with figures and she's always helped Dad in the business,' she told him. It was a labour of love, always had been and she knew that her mother did not receive a proper salary for her contribution but until recently she seemed to enjoy just being there once or twice a week.

'She's retired then?'

'Don't say that. She's not sixty yet but I think she just got tired of it.'

She was regretting her impulsive decision to invite Brian for Christmas for, to be honest, they didn't know each other that well, had jumped into bed far too soon and a relationship based purely on sex was on a hiding to nothing. There had to be more to it than that. She suspected her parents were delighted that she had asked somebody along at last, her mother already acting as if this was it and that a wedding would be in the offing before long.

'They'll like you,' she went on quickly. 'And don't take any notice if my mother starts to quiz you. It's just her way.'

'I thought you said it was your father who would be quizzing me?'

'Both of them, I'm afraid. I don't see them very often and they want to know everything that's been going on since the last time. As you are something new I'm afraid you're for it. My mother's interrogation technique is second to none. She'll know more about you in half an hour than I've found out in three months.'

It was a gentle dig but for once he did not respond negatively.

'I can handle that,' he said displaying that confidence

that she liked about him. 'I'm looking forward to meeting everybody, Amy. I have nobody to call family so it's interesting to know how these things operate.'

'Oh no, that sounds ominous.' She kept her voice light although something was niggling at her. 'I hope it won't be too much of an ordeal. My brother and I usually come to blows.'

'Why is that?'

'We're just too different. It's not unusual. It's a brother and sister thing,' she added with a smile.

He returned her smile, reached for her hand and squeezed it, which made her feel a lot better. Christmas always did this to her, put her on edge, and she knew she should just learn to relax and enjoy it for once. Maybe Monique was right; maybe she did take life much too seriously. She was not going to allow Monique to annoy her, not this time, but she would have to remind herself to count to ten before she said the wrong thing. She always spoke too soon where that little lady was concerned. Monique had perfected the art of looking as if she was about to burst into tears, a look that tore at the heart of any man. It was a useful trait but not one she could emulate. Amy did not cry often but when she did it was the genuine article and she preferred to do it alone because the heaving shoulders, the funny strangled gulping sounds, snot-filled nose, and panda eyes that accompanied her crying was not pretty to behold. Just now, as she sat in the car in front of the house she knew as home, a little stirring inside came as a warning that, emotionally, the sight of it affected her deeply, so she quickly sniffed away the slightest hint of that, reverting to the brisk and business-like exterior she liked to present to the world.

'It's only a flying visit anyway,' she went on, trying to reassure herself as much as Brian. 'I can't afford to take much time off at this time of year. We open up again the day after Boxing Day but I'm giving that one a miss. We shan't rest until we've got the sales over.'

'Don't talk shop.'

'Sorry.' He was, she knew, becoming increasingly impatient with that and she vowed not to mention the store again over the next couple of days although she could not guarantee that nobody else would. Their arrival had surely been noticed and suddenly she was anxious to get the introductions over. Maybe, if she was lucky, she might actually enjoy the break. 'Come on.' She clambered out and slammed the car door, stretching and smiling towards the house that was still home.

'I would never have guessed that the removal business could be so lucrative,' Brian said, helping her lift their cases and the Christmas gifts out of the boot.

'It's holding its own although things are not easy just now. My grandfather started the business off with just one van,' she told him proudly. 'And then he was lucky to get a council contract way back in the sixties and that really helped him build things up. My father's just carried it on and eventually, I suppose, my brother will take over.'

'Lucky brother,' he said with an easy smile but she glanced sharply at him all the same. He had stayed overnight at her place last night. She had prepared a meal or at least bought something from the luxury range at M&S and followed the cooking instructions to the letter. They had demolished a bottle of Merlot between them and afterwards had snuggled up beside the fire – gas, unfortunately, not a lovely log one – watching a romantic comedy on television and eventually gone to bed. Compared with his place her flat was tiny, the bedroom scarcely big enough for the bed and she was very aware that the walls were thin and that she had neighbours.

He certainly knew what was what, saying and doing all the right things, and she knew she should feel fabulous and loved but something was missing and frankly, as she awoke this morning and hastily got out of bed before it all started up again, she was having serious second thoughts. It just wasn't doing it for her. It was fun, sexy, a good excuse to treat herself to some pretty underwear and she hadn't done this sort of thing for a while so it was all new again; a guilty pleasure.

And yet, aside from the more than passable sex, the way he kept buttoned up about his private life and indeed his work was becoming increasingly concerning. He had money, dressed well and drove a brand new black Mercedes; he had a fantastic house filled with expensive furniture and furnishings and he bought and sold collectibles, art and antiques. That was Brian. Trying to get any more information out of him was a lost cause akin to chipping away at concrete with a penknife and it was beginning to rattle her.

And another thing that was bothering her, one that she had hinted about on the journey, was the lack of family paraphernalia. Everybody had family of sorts but looking round his place it was like a show home with no personal items whatsoever aside from his choice of paintings of which there were many. Somebody had done the interior for him and although the whole place was beautifully warm, heated with a state-of-the-art underfloor system there was a chill about it, too.

Perhaps it needed a female touch but she had an uncomfortable feeling it would not be her. Pleasing Janet was not a reason to keep this thing on-going. She just knew it wasn't fair on him if he thought this relationship was going anywhere. There was no mention of marriage or indeed the serious commitment of moving in together for they had only known each other a short time but neither of them was that young and at their age things could turn serious pretty damned quickly. Her whole life could change in an instant on the toss of a coin or perhaps the glimmer of a diamond ring. She knew that if he asked her that question just now she would say no or more likely she would stall and ask for time to think about it. Moving into that lovely barn conversion was tempting and she would not miss her little flat one little bit but that was hardly the right reason to accept a proposal of marriage.

Was she making a big mistake in bringing him here? You only introduced somebody into the family if you were moderately serious, didn't you? And was her motive in doing so just to shut her mother up? Janet thought Brian was wonderful but she had only met him the once and she was going purely on physical looks and the winning way he seemed to have with the older ladies. Increasingly, she was beginning to doubt her judgement when it came to Brian and she wondered sometimes just what his hold on her was and how long she would put up with it.

Too late now, for they were here now and she would have to make the best of it.

She aimed the remote at the car, clicked it. 'There's Mum. Come and meet her.'

Chapter Five

Christine was pinning a lot of hope on Brian.

It had been a big surprise, a shock even, when Amy had phoned and asked if she could bring a friend along for Christmas. She could sense her daughter's anxiety and was quick to reassure her that they would be delighted to meet the friend, a man called Brian.

She knew nothing about Brian yet but she determined that over the course of the next few days she would find out the lot. Amy had had only a few boyfriends over the years, was never one for flitting between men, thoroughly focused as she was both at school and university, although of course Christine was not privy to what might have gone on there. It is a funny time when you send your children off to university, grown up kids in theory, but there was that pang in letting them go into that big bad world. It was a disappointment but also a relief when Mike did not get good enough grades because she felt he was the kind of person to be more easily led than Amy whom she was confident could stand her ground with the best of them. Amy was a bright young lady and not easily intimidated, as had been proved. She was proud of her but she worried that her daughter was missing out on the things that mattered in life and that one day, when it was much too late, she would finally cotton on to that and look back with regret.

Amy was late arriving and those familiar mother-nerves

kicked in, her imagination on overdrive as the minutes passed with no answer from Amy's phone. So the relief was great as she saw the little yellow car coming up the drive at last. She waited a moment, hidden behind the curtain in the dining room as the two of them got out, retrieving bags and wrapped presents from the boot. The first thing she noticed was that Amy had had her dark brown hair cut short; the elfin style suited her. She was a striking girl who had always had unfounded doubts about her appearance, tall and strong-looking, very much her father's daughter with her light brown wide-set eyes and, not visible but there all the same, his steely determination to succeed.

She saw at once that Brian was an attractive-looking man, about the same height as Amy with fairish hair, wearing jeans over tan boots and a leather biker-style jacket, an outfit that seemed altogether too young for him, for at first glance she saw he was older than Amy by maybe as much as ten years. She saw him leaning in towards her, caught the smiles they exchanged, which confirmed what she had expected – that the two of them were very close.

Frank was less happy than she was about the unexpected guest.

'What do we know about this guy?' he asked when she informed him, going straight into overprotective father mode.

'Nothing, yet.'

'She must be serious about him if she's bringing him to meet us. She's never brought anybody home before, has she?'

'Yes she has. There was that lovely boy at school,' Christine said, recalling that, like her own parents, she had hoped something might come of that one. He was from such a nice family and because she liked him and his family so much she had kept track of him over the years. He became a doctor and was married now with three children living away from his home town. Occasionally she met his mother and they chatted about him and Amy, never quite saying what they were both thinking.

'What boy?'

Clearly Frank's memory was not as good as hers or maybe he had never seen the potential there.

'Never mind.' She shrugged it off.

'What does this man do? How long has she known him?'

'I've told you. I don't know. She's thirty-five, Frank, not a teenager and she's a good judge of character. He'll be fine, you'll see.'

But now, as Amy came smilingly towards her, the man following, Christine had a sudden unexpected and totally bizarre reaction.

For reasons she could not decipher, as he took hold of her hand and smiled at her, she took an instant dislike to him.

It could snow all it liked now that Amy was here and wouldn't you know it, as the afternoon progressed it did just that. The forecast had promised snow for the last week and indeed there had been a brief flurry the day before but it had not settled.

Christine showed Amy and Brian up to their rooms, feeling stupidly flustered as they stood in what was earmarked as Brian's room pointing out the interlocking door. She caught the slightest smile from him as she explained about the shared bathroom arrangements between this room and Amy's and was reminded of one of her son's school friends whom she had never taken to either who had, not surprisingly at all, turned out to be a rotten apple in every respect. As she grew older and wiser, she was rarely wrong about men but hoped in this case she was for he was the first adult man Amy had brought home and Frank was quite right, for that must mean something.

'Do make yourself at home, Brian' she said, pointing out the wardrobe and chest of drawers as if he couldn't see these damned huge pieces of furniture for himself before giving him a run-down on how the radiators worked.

'Mum, stop fussing, we can adjust a radiator,' Amy laughed, giving her a quick hug. 'And it's boiling in here, anyway.'

'We like to keep the heating on otherwise it's like that ice hotel I've seen on television. Have you seen that, Brian? You actually lie on a bed shaped from ice. You have warm furs to cover you, of course, and candles and it's all rather lovely….' She tailed off, knowing she was rambling on about nothing because she was nervous. 'If you need anything else just give me a shout,' she finished, wishing she could stop acting like a B&B owner.

Leaving Brian to unpack in his room she followed Amy through to the adjoining one. All the bedrooms were a good size and this was no exception, with the addition of an elegant modern chandelier hanging from the high ceiling. It was a well-proportioned room with a brass-framed double bed dressed with simple pale blue linen so that it was feminine without being too girly. A comfortable armchair covered in a blue floral fabric was turned towards the window and the view of the rear garden that sloped gently down to the river. The view was softened when the trees were in leaf but today with the branches bare they could see beyond the river and over to a cluster of houses on the opposite bank towards the hill that dominated the village. Snow was falling steadily now and it looked as if it might settle.

'It looks just the same,' Amy said, taking a moment to stand and stare.

'Exactly. Why change something when it's perfect?'

'You'll miss this place if you have to leave.'

'Why would we leave? We have no intention of leaving.'

'Oh come on, Mum, it's too big for just the two of you.'

'It was too big for the four of us.' Christine changed the subject abruptly. 'He seems very nice,' she said, lowering her voice and smiling brightly, watching as Amy placed her suitcase on the bed and opened it. She noticed how neatly it was packed but that was no surprise, for Amy liked to keep things tidy. 'How long have you known him?'

'Since September.' Amy ran her fingers through her hair, looking surprised as she caught sight of herself in the mirror. 'This is a mistake. I'm going to let it grow again. I can't get used to it like this.'

Ah. So she wasn't keen to talk about Brian. Sensing the rebuff, Christine determined she would not allow it to upset her. It would all come out, in bits and pieces, and she could observe them together and come to her own conclusion.

'I like your hair like that and it's lovely to have you here, sweetheart, even if it's only for a few days.' She hoped that didn't sound like a criticism but honestly you would have thought she could have got a few more days off as they hadn't seen her since August, just before she met this man. She knew that it was partly their fault as she did not relish the trip down to Leeds. Amy's flat was poky and they had to stay in a hotel and after a few days she was left with the distinct impression that their daughter would be glad to see the back of them as they were causing serious disruptions to her routine.

'A few days off is the best I can manage,' Amy said without a trace of regret or apology. 'You've no idea how busy it is just now. We need our Christmas figures to be a big improvement on last year so it's make or break time. It's a tough business, Mum.'

'I know.' She very nearly said that perhaps it might have been easier if she had stuck to what she had known from childhood. Amy knew all there was to know about the removal business, had gone into the office with her dad when she was quite young to 'learn the ropes' because they had always known that getting Mike motivated would be a challenge.

And so it had proved. Frank had come close to sacking him but she had persuaded him otherwise for how on earth could they live with themselves if they did that? As it was, his job description was vague in the extreme and the rest of the workforce did not know quite what to make of him, unsure if they should treat him as one of the lads or the boss-to-be?

'Are you missing the office?' Amy asked. 'I was surprised when Dad said you had walked out on him.'

'Did he tell you that?' She knew that Frank rang Amy more than she did although he rarely bothered to tell her when he did so. 'I didn't walk out on him. What a daft thing to say. I've been threatening to do it for ages so it came as no surprise.' She laughed. 'I might have been only going in a couple of times a week but I suddenly realized I was working twice as hard as everybody else. I was just paid a token wage because I needed to be on the books.'

'I told you that was a mistake. You should have paid yourself a proper salary, Mum, otherwise you're just fooling around with the figures.' Her eyes narrowed. 'Is Shirley still bossing everybody about? Dad's allowed that woman to get too big for her boots and I was never that impressed with her. She forgets things.'

'Your father likes her and she's been there for ever.' She had to put a stop to this conversation as it was always difficult to talk about Shirley. She didn't really believe Frank was having an affair but it wasn't for want of Shirley trying. She was one of those women who enter a room bosom first. 'I'll leave you to unpack, darling. Come down when you're ready.'

Now, some time later as she brought a pot of coffee and mince pies through to the drawing room, the flakes were becoming bolder and starting to lie.

Perfect. It was Christmas Eve and most people would now be where they needed to be so travel disruption would be at a minimum. In any case, even though it was a selfish thought, her little family was safe so that was all that mattered.

She looked happily around the room trying to visualize it through Brian's eyes. It was difficult to achieve a cosy feel in a room this size and it was maybe a touch cluttered for the modern man but frankly she did not care. She loved it and that was all that mattered.

'Look, it's snowing,' Amy said delightedly, turning to Brian who was sitting beside her on the sofa. 'I love snow. One winter when we were little we made a snowman and it was so cold that he stayed out there for weeks.'

'Days, sweetheart, don't exaggerate.' Frank was burrowing into the drinks cupboard. 'We've got the lot here. Do you fancy a drink, Brian?'

'I'm fine just now with coffee, thanks.'

'Mike and Monique will be here soon,' Christine said, settling herself down. Amy had commented on the tree, said it looked lovely and silvery, which had made Christine shoot Frank a triumphant look. The fire was lit with the log basket stacked high and now that all the Christmas food was bought in, sitting in the refrigerator and freezer, and the larder shelves were heaving with extra items, Christine could at last relax.

She had a new flatteringly draped red dress for tomorrow and she had the silly hats ready for them to wear for the Christmas day meal although she was not sure about them, wondered if that little tradition should be dropped, especially with a newcomer at the table. Brian did not look as if he would be comfortable wearing a pirate's hat.

She tried to signal a warning to Frank across the room, wondered what his initial reaction to Brian had been for they had not been alone since his arrival, wondered also when the interrogation would start.

'So what do you do with yourself, Brian?' Frank said, swirling the whisky round his glass before taking a sip but not before he flashed Christine a mischievous glance.

'I run my own business, Frank,' Brian said after a moment.

Brian had jumped in immediately with first names, not something Frank was necessarily used to but, if he was surprised, he did not show it. Christine was much more relaxed about such things and would have instantly corrected him if he had addressed her as Mrs Fletcher. She was worried about her initial reaction to him but then she had always done that with people, formed an instant impression and it had to be said that her instincts were usually right. She had taken to Monique at once, for instance, and what a delightful uncomplicated daughter-in-law she was proving to be.

'You say you run your own business?' Frank said easily but not before Christine spotted the slightest smile Amy and Brian exchanged. 'What line are you in?'

'Art and antiques,' Brian said with a quick look around. 'You have some interesting items.'

'My parents had a good eye and a lot of these pieces belonged to them.' Christine said, standing up to pass round the plate of warm mince pies and the linen napkins, taking the opportunity to shoot her husband a warning glance. No more questions please.

'Must be difficult at the moment, this moving lark,' Brian commented, turning the tables on him. 'Everybody's staying put so far as I can make out. And nobody can afford to buy a house, not at today's prices. I'm glad I bought my property a few years ago when it was a bit easier.'

'Do you live in Leeds, then?' Christine asked with a smile, feeling it was an easier subject.

'I live out in the sticks, on the outskirts of Wetherby.'

'Brian lives in a converted barn, Mum,' Amy told her. 'It's beautiful. It's enormous and very modern.'

'How lovely.' She had a vision of soaring ceilings and stripped pine floors. Converted barns with no cosy corners were not her thing at all but she was in no hurry to confess that and it was a relief, therefore, when the bell rang and Mike's voice rang out to announce their arrival. She hurried out into the hall to greet them.

Chapter Six

They walked up from their house carrying the presents, for it seemed daft to use the car particularly as the snow was heavier now, falling in fat flakes, and the drive at Snape House was steep with an awkward curve halfway up.

'I think we should leave it until after Christmas to tell them,' Mike said as they set out. They had discussed this over and over and kept changing their minds as to when it would be the right moment or if indeed there would ever be a right moment. 'It would be a shame to spoil things. You know how much Mum loves Christmas and all the fuss.'

'You're probably right.' Monique could see the little puffs of air as they exhaled and, shivering, she pulled the hood of her jacket up, clumpy multi-laced boots poking out from under her long skirt. The sky was heavily laden with snow clouds, darkness fast approaching and everyday sounds were already becoming muffled as the snow settled softly around them. They were not staying over even though Christine had offered and now Monique wished they had taken up the invitation for she did not relish a late-night trudge back through what might be a significant snowfall, not in this footwear, although Christine would no doubt lend her a pair of Wellington boots.

'We'll stay tonight if it gets any worse,' Mike said, reading her mind. 'If I know Mum, the bed will be made up just in case.'

'But I like my own bed best,' she murmured, thinking of their high-sided French inspired bed with its sumptuously soft mattress, goose-feather pillows and super warm duvet. It was little more than a large single in order to fit into the little room but that suited them fine. Aunt Sylvie was right, French women knew all there was to know about the marriage bed and keeping the husband happy and maybe taking a lover was no bad thing. Her sex life, the safely married part, had been taken up a notch recently and although Mike was thrilled he had yet to know the reason why. Comparison was an ugly thing but she could not avoid it and happily, after all the soul searching of late, it was Mike not Sol who was making it happen for her now. As they headed for Snape House she knew that she had to end it with Sol once and for all before Mike found out and it all went pear-shaped. She would see Sol one more time and end it. It had to be done in person; writing a letter was not only cowardly but also dangerous as was the alternative – a text message – and a phone call would just end in tears.

It was nice while it lasted but, come on, surely he had known from the beginning that it would be short lived. She had tried to end it on several occasions but although she started off full of good intentions Sol refused to take her seriously, laughing her excuses away and, to her irritation every single time she had ended up having sex with him, supposedly for the very last time.

'Hey, watch it.' Mike grabbed her as she slid on a slippery patch. 'We don't want you breaking a leg.'

'It would cause havoc, wouldn't it?' Redistributing the presents, she freed a hand so that she could hold onto him, her nose nipped by the cold.

'You never know, if we can get here for next Christmas there might be three of us,' Mike said, squeezing her hand through her gloves.

'There might.' She smiled into the darkness. She was sorry to disappoint him, over and over, but he would get over it and the last thing she wanted was a child.

'It's a surprise, isn't it, that Amy's bringing somebody along,' she said, switching to a safer subject. 'Christine's very excited about it. She thinks it must be serious.'

'I hope she doesn't frighten him off.'

'She won't. She didn't frighten *me* off,' she said, recalling how welcoming Christine had been but then she had worked out beforehand how to play the nervous newcomer to perfection. Christine wore her heart on her sleeve, which made her very easy to read. 'I wonder what Brian will be like?

'God only knows but he's a saint in my book to take Amy on. Maybe he likes bossy women.'

'Be nice to her, please.' She caught the little grumble from him. 'I know what you two are like. It might have been funny when you are little but you're grown up now and you should stop the teasing.'

'She asks for it,' he said. 'She acts like she runs that store when I bet she's only a general dogsbody. She puts me down all the time and she's willing me to fail because everybody knows she could do the job standing on her head. *And*, the thing I really can't forgive her for is that she turns her nose up at your paintings.'

She pulled him to a halt, still in the part of the drive that was not visible from the house itself. 'Let it go. It's Christmas. We don't want a repeat of last year not when we have a visitor.'

'If he's serious about her then he'll have to get used to it,' Mike grinned. 'It's just brother and sister stuff.'

'In that case I'm glad I don't have a brother.' She stamped her feet, feeling the cold, blowing away a snowflake that had settled on her face. 'I am not moving an inch, Mike, until you promise to behave.'

'Scout's honour.' He had a lovely smile, one of the things she found attractive about him, that and his voice. He was of a stocky build like his father but he managed to keep just the right side of a weight problem but he had to take care for it could easily go wrong. An interesting-looking scar just below the eye was the result of a childhood mishap but it added character and the first time she met him she found her eyes drawn constantly to it. Now she scarcely noticed.

The house looked welcoming with its lights on and smoke puffing out of the chimney. The outside decorative lamp post was glowing, sending yellowy streams of light across the drive, illuminating the bank of shrubs near the entrance and giving them a strange ghost-like quality as the first of the snow settled upon them. The gravel closest to the door was only thinly covered as yet, the little stones sparkling in the light. There was a holly wreath fastened to the door, a solid door that afforded no glimpse of the hall beyond.

They would open the presents this evening, a tradition in their family long before they discovered the Royals did that too and then there would be a board game, God help the new man. She and Mike would get away hopefully before midnight, returning tomorrow for Christmas lunch.

They reached the porch and stamped their feet free of most of the snow before Mike opened the door to announce their arrival. Monique unlaced her boots leaving them in the porch, slipping her feet into the red ballerina pumps she had brought with her.

Stepping inside, Monique caught sight of herself in the large mirror over the hall table, approving of what she saw. She loved vintage clothes, liked to be just that little bit different and tonight she was wearing one of her favourite skirts; a black floral net with a stiff black under-slip attached to it and a cream twin-set, a double row of pearls completing the look. She did not possess a single pair of trousers and even in bed she preferred Victorian-style white cotton nightgowns to pyjamas. With the frilly bits, they were impossible to iron but again she could not bear to go to bed in anything other than a crisply ironed nightdress. Tonight she wore her hair loose and it hung like shimmering golden curtains from its centre parting. After the walk in the cold night air, she was a little flushed, as was Mike.

She gave him a fond glance as they gently deposited the presents in the hall before taking off their outdoor things.

The door to the drawing room opened and Christine came smilingly through to greet them.

Monique was her usual breathless self, the childlike quality every bit as annoying as ever. Amy did her best to try to understand the woman, goodness knows, but she found women like Monique such hard work. Airy fairy was the kindest way to describe it; she wouldn't last five minutes in the cut-throat world of retail.

Her brother and his wife must be the only couple in England who didn't have a television and didn't they like to go on about that? She had warned Brian what to expect but even so the sight of Monique bouncing into the room wearing the weirdest black skirt and Grace Kelly-type twin-set took him by surprise. She was barely five feet tall and the ballerina-like shoes did nothing to help. She wore not a trace of make-up, of course, which would cause Bea in Cosmetics to have a fit although it had to be said that Monique's pale skin was as close to perfect as it was possible to be and her hair, naturally blonde, would you believe, was glossy and beautiful.

The contrast to her own short locks was alarming and not, she felt, to her advantage. Monique, small and slender and exquisitely pretty, was like a doll compared to her and she made her feel extra tall and extra bulky.

Kisses were exchanged and the likelihood of the snow lying was discussed at some length with Monique standing in the middle of the room directly below the centre light as if she was on stage. At Amy's side Brian was unusually quiet but then Monique did have that effect on men – it must be the French blood and that coy sideways look from those big grey eyes heavily fringed with long lashes. Who needed mascara with lashes like those? Bea would be on cloud nine if she got her hands on Monique, reaching gleefully for the palette of shadows and liners to enhance those eyes. Funnily though, the natural look was much more effective.

Christine sped off into the kitchen to finish off what she had told them was a simple Christmas Eve meal and Monique chose to squeeze herself between Amy and Brian, turning her attention firstly to Amy. A light perfume, delightful and subtle, rose from her like a cloud, contrasting with the heavier fragrance of 'Bella-Sophia', which, for all its hype, Amy had still not made up her mind about.

'You poor darling. You must be shattered,' she said, taking in every detail of Amy's appearance in one swift glance. 'I went into Preston last week and it was horrendous. The shops were heaving.'

'It has been busy,' Amy admitted with a smile. 'And it isn't finished yet. We have the sales starting in a couple of days.'

'No wonder you look so tired,' Monique's smile seemed sincere but it was a sly put-down for all that. Amy had refreshed her make-up before Mike and Monique arrived so she had thought she had successfully disguised the fact that the frantic activity of the past two weeks was finally catching up on her. She felt she could sleep for a week and last night's bedtime activity had not helped. Even now, she was hard put not to yawn, putting up a hand across her mouth to stifle the impulse.

'Well, yes, but then working for your living is quite hard,' she said, cross to be saying it; it was uncalled for, drawing attention as it did to the fact that Monique did not have an actual job.

'I work too,' she pouted looking so hurt that Amy felt herself flush as Brian glanced sharply at her. 'Don't I, Mike?'

'Monique's a brilliant artist,' Mike said, also giving Amy a look and making her feel as nasty as the Wicked Witch of the West.

'Of course you are. Sorry,' she muttered, smiling an apology. 'I'm just tired that's all and a bit snappy.'

'I can vouch for that,' Brian said with a grin, the glib remark offending her deeply because when had she been snappy with him? 'So you're an artist, Monique? That is very interesting. I've always wanted to be able to paint.' Brian was all ears and with Monique giving her the cold shoulder Amy felt superfluous, exchanging a glance with her father, who merely shook his head in warning. If she looked tired then he did too and she worried for him. It might well have been only a little scare but nevertheless it was a warning they ought not to ignore. She knew he was difficult and she knew that she had let him down, too, because he had really wanted her to go into the business but at least he understood and respected her decision, which was more than her mother did.

Amy stifled a sigh. Again it must be the French blood but her dear sister-in-law was a dreadful flirt and she just knew even without seeing it that she was giving Brian the full benefit of that shy yet sensuous look she had perfected.

'What's your speciality?' Brian asked and Amy could not be sure if he was genuinely interested or just making polite conversation. 'I'm always on the look-out for original artwork.'

'Really?' She shot a glance at Mike. 'Did you hear that, darling?'

'Yes, well perhaps you can show Brian some of your work later,' Amy said hoping to snip this topic of conversation in the bud. She had no talent for drawing, just as she couldn't cook, and most importantly of all she could not do the sweet little woman thing that Monique was so good at. And to top all this she was annoyed at herself for reacting in this way. She was being an absolute cow. It was totally unjustified and not worthy of her to think badly of Monique and she had no idea why she did it but she just did. Perhaps it was the way her mother hung on to Monique's every word; perhaps there was even an element of jealousy lingering there, for sometimes it seemed that her mother thought more about Monique than her. Even her telephone calls were littered with 'Monique this, Monique that'. As soon as a pregnancy was announced that would be it. When that happened, when there was a Fletcher baby in the offing, Amy might as well not exist in her mother's books. Her earlier good mood of girlish pre-Christmas excitement was rapidly diminishing, tiredness taking over and making her act like this.

'Amy, darling, give me a hand, would you?' Christine appeared at the door waving a wooden spoon and looking uncharacteristically flustered.

'No, you're tired, Amy. You sit and talk to Mike,' Monique said, leaping up in one graceful movement and stepping daintily over Brian's outstretched feet. 'On my way, Christine.'

Amy gave a shrug, not too unhappy about it, knowing she might well be a liability in the kitchen. Her mother's idea of a simple meal had to be seen to be believed. She had already caught a glimpse of the preparations in the kitchen and there seemed to be an awful lot going on. She had also peeped into the dining room; the table was looking splendid but then her mother certainly knew how to entertain.

'Long time no see,' Mike said cheerfully, sitting opposite her. In direct contrast to hers, he had let his hair grow and in Amy's opinion it was too long, dark like hers, the scar on his face as noticeable as ever. She hoped nobody mentioned it for that would mean everybody looking at her and shaking their heads as if she could be held responsible. She was only a child when it happened and it was an accident. She never meant to hurt him and it was mortifying that the scar should remain as a permanent reminder of her fit of temper.

'Long time no see,' she echoed. 'You look well, Mike.'

'Wish I could say the same. You look knackered, sis. You work too hard, that's your problem.'

'Don't call me sis,' she felt irritation bubbling up already and they had only spoken a few words. 'And you would be knackered, too, if you'd been working non-stop for the past two weeks. A department store in the run up to Christmas is not the place to be, believe me.'

'Oh I don't know, it's been fairly hectic for us, too.' Mike glanced at their father. 'Hasn't it, Dad? I went down to Kent with the guys to help with a big move. It was a two-van DBDA affair because they had a lot of antiques and two crates of fragiles. They were a crusty pair, eagle-eyed, standing over us as we unpacked and we didn't want any cock-ups. It was a tricky one, terrible staircase, but we got them installed without any problems.' He looked again at his father, maybe expecting a nod of approval but not getting it.

'DBDA?' Brian queried.

'Don't bloody drop anything,' Mike replied with a grin. 'Or we'd be onto insurance claims even before you picked it up.'

'Did you get a decent tip?' Frank asked. 'You can usually suss out the folk who are going to be mean buggers when it comes to the tip.'

'That would be me then. I don't agree with tips,' Brian said, the remark sinking like a stone as Frank's raised eyebrows showed his surprise. 'On principle, I never give tips.'

Amy had, somewhat to her embarrassment, already noticed that. At a restaurant recently she had surreptitiously found a crumpled ten pound note to deposit on the table as they left after she realized that a tip was not forthcoming from Brian. The service had been excellent so she saw no reason at all to withhold one. It was a little thing but somehow important. If Brian noticed the sudden change in mood of the other two men he pretended not to, carrying on blissfully.

'So you do a bit of hands-on stuff then, Mike?' he asked, stretching out an arm as if to put it round Amy's shoulders. A little annoyed at the way he had reacted to Monique she childishly moved away as he did so, so that it ended up just trailing along the edge of the sofa.

'To know a business you have to start at the bottom and work up,' Frank said, looking odd to Amy without the customary cigarette lodged between his lips. 'Only then can you look a guy in the eye who's doing the rough stuff. If you've been there, done that, then they respect you that bit more. We can all drive the vans, carry furniture, do packing, dismantle and reassemble, you name it. Even Amy has an HGV licence.'

'Has she?' Brian glanced at her. 'You didn't say.'

'It's not the sort of thing that comes up in conversation,' she said.

'Well, well....' he seemed amused. 'No wonder you don't like people to criticize your driving!'

Mike laughed. 'Don't tell me you're guilty of that, Brian? You're on dangerous ground there. Even though I say it myself, she's one of the best drivers I know.'

'Thanks.' She shot a grateful glance his way and he winked at her.

It was all genial enough but she was sensitive to her family's mood and she knew without asking that Brian was going down like a lead balloon.

Before it could get any worse, her mother popped her head round the door to announce that dinner was ready.

'It's nothing too exciting,' she said, already in apologetic mode for what Amy knew would be a fantastic meal. 'I'm doing beef tomorrow so I thought we would settle for something simple tonight. It's just something I've rustled up – a fish pie with a difference and a homemade strawberry meringue to follow. Hope you like fish, Brian?'

'I do, thank you.'

Amy caught his rueful smile. She knew he hated fish and it was nice of him not to make a fuss about it. This was the problem with him. He was ever so slightly Jekyll and Hyde. His manner sometimes verged on arrogant and rude but then he had the ability of shaking that off and being very pleasant. He was certainly trying hard with her mother but she was not sure just what her mum was making of that for she was nowhere near as gullible as Janet.

They moved into the dining room and took their seats. As they did so, she caught the look Mike and Monique exchanged; a secretive half-smile on both their lips.

Something was up and the only thing she could come up with was that Monique was finally pregnant. At least if she was and they announced it over dinner that would be the prime topic of conversation for the next few days and the heat would be off her and Brian.

Chapter Seven

Embarrassingly, Brian's Christmas gift was not to her taste but she thought she made a good show of enthusiasm for it. Her present to him was a sweater, bought rather guiltily from one of their competitors' stores simply because she felt she ought to; buying any of her presents with her staff discount seemed a bit off.

Mike and Monique bought her a voucher for a spa treatment. 'You look as if you're in desperate need of it,' Monique said on handing it over. 'You'll be able to relax and let all your worries drift away.'

'Thanks, Monique. That's very thoughtful.'

It was pointless saying she had no worries.

'Thanks for the shirt, darling,' her father said later, catching her in the family room where she had wandered in search of some quiet time to browse through the old and much-read books.

'Sorry if it was a bit boring,' she said, smiling at him. 'You must think I have no imagination at all.'

'Nonsense. I always need shirts.'

She sat down on a familiar chair. 'They won't think we're being unsociable will they if we stay in here a while?'

'Shouldn't think so. Monique is keeping that man of yours entertained.'

She noted the 'that man of yours', recognized the doubts

in his voice. He sat down opposite her and smiled and she relaxed at last. It was ridiculous but they rarely got the chance to be alone these days and so these moments were precious and to be treasured.

'How are you, sweetheart?' he asked quietly. 'You look tired. I hope you're not overdoing things.'

'Hard work never killed anybody,' she said, regretting that remark as soon as she uttered it. 'At least—'

'Hard work didn't cause my problem,' he told her. 'I'm afraid a dicky heart runs in the family. Your mother made too much of it and, look at me, I'm absolutely fine. Never felt better, as a matter of fact, now that I've passed the MOT with the doctor.'

She did not argue.

'Do you like Brian?' she asked and she knew that it was a ridiculous question to ask and instantly waved her hand as if she was retracting it. 'Don't answer.'

'I have to reserve judgement,' he said quietly and truthfully. 'But if he makes you happy, darling, then that's fine by me.'

'It's not serious, Dad,' she told him, needing him to know that. 'I don't know why I brought him along. I can't see it going anywhere. He's all right but he irritates me to hell.'

'And he doesn't give tips.' Her father shook his head. 'He'd better not visit the States then or he'd be in real trouble.'

'I'll talk to him about it. There must be a reason because he's not short of money.'

'It's a bit of an ordeal for the chap coming here to meet the family. I shall never forget meeting Monique for the first time. She looked about twelve years old, had her hair in a plait for God's sake.'

They shared a gentle smile. Enough said.

'Give it a chance,' he continued amiably. 'There's no such thing as the perfect man, you know. Ask your mother.' His sudden grin was infectious and she laughed with him. He rarely let off steam and she knew she was like him, firmly embedded in the serious side of life, craving perfection in both her private and working life and knowing that it would not happen. Something somewhere had to give. She had worried when she was younger that all was not well with her parents' marriage but that was because so many of her friends' parents were splitting up, but she was now satisfied that hers would stay together, that the crisp familiarity they shared was just their way. They did not seem overly affectionate towards each other but they had been married a long time and she supposed that happened. Suddenly, though, she had a vision of her future, knew that she would be crazy to enter into a relationship with somebody about whom she already had grave doubts but knew also that she did not want to be alone forever. She loved her career – how she loved it – but how would she feel twenty years on?

'But do you like him, Dad?' she persisted and it was suddenly important that she got a positive answer.

'Don't put me on the spot. I don't know him yet. Aside from the fact that he's a mean bugger he seems okay.'

'I'm thirty-five,' she said, looking across to the bookshelves and seeing some old favourites there. 'No spring chicken as they say.'

'*Who* says? You're only a child.'

'Hardly.' She sighed, turning to face him. 'How's life with you these days? How are you feeling?'

'Okay.' He hesitated only a moment. 'I've been better, I suppose. It was scary.'

'How's the business?'

'So so, and we'll get through this rough patch as soon as the housing market picks up.'

'You've taken a nose dive this year, then?'

He shook his head. 'It's not as bad as that. People still move house whatever the state of the economy but we've had to hold our prices in order to stay competitive, and throw in a few discounts as well, and that all eats into the profits. Anyway, I don't want you to be worried about it. We'll get by.'

She didn't want to talk business, didn't want to upset him, and she didn't like to admit to herself that he looked different. The illness had aged him and it was as if a sparkle had fizzled out. He had never been the life-and-soul-of-the-party type but the two of them had always shared something special, something that was missing between her and her mother.

'I could always come back into the business if you'd have me,' she said as the thought struck her. 'I'm not sure what's happening with my job in the New Year.'

'So you want to hedge your bets? You would be very welcome, darling, although I don't know how Mike would react to it. What the hell am I going to do with him, Amy? I can't sack my own son, your mother's made that quite clear, but I tell you, if he was anybody other than my son he would have been long gone.'

'As bad as that?'

'As bad as that. I worry about what will happen when I'm gone.' He looked suddenly so much older. 'Don't tell your mother. But I have an awful feeling that my days are numbered. After all, my grandfather and then my dad both died young so the odds are stacked against me. I'm doing everything I should be doing, more or less, but you never know what's round the corner.'

'Hey, come on.' She went across to him and cuddled into him feeling his arms slipping round her. He was wearing a cashmere sweater and it was comfortably soft. Underneath she could hear his heart beating, nice and regular, thank heavens, and he smelt of soap with just a trace of cigarettes thrown in, which was what he meant by the 'more or less'. 'What is it about Christmas that makes everybody so bloody depressed?'

'Less of the swearing, young lady,' he pushed her gently away, smiling now.

There was the sound of laughter from the other room and the television blared forth.

'We'd better go back in or they'll wonder where we are.'

'I miss you when you're not here,' he said wistfully. 'You should come to see us more often. One thing more....'

'What?'

'All I want is for you to be happy. Don't let your mother drive you into doing something you don't want to do.'

'Are you warning me off Brian? I've told you, Dad, it's not serious.'

'Then why the hell is he here?'

Following him out of the room, she wondered that too.

Brian slipped into Amy's bed in the early hours of Christmas morning, shaking her out of the dream she was engaged in. In the dream she was at the store although, as in the way of dreams, it was a mixture of the various ones she had worked in. She was running late but on coming into the store through Cosmetics & Perfumery there was Bea looking as if she had just woken up; hair messy, face shiny, in old cotton pyjamas, pink fur-trimmed granny slippers. She yanked Amy's arm as she passed muttering that she didn't want Daniel to see her like this. Amy had never seen Bea looking so vulnerable and that was when she awoke to see Brian, eyes full of expectation, beside her. He was wearing boxers but no top and already, even though she was only half awake his hands were sliding up her leg.

'Happy Christmas,' he murmured against her ear. 'I thought it would be a nice way to start the day.'

'For heaven's sake, do you know what time it is?' She pushed him aside and peered at the bedside clock. 'A quarter to two, that's what.'

'I thought you'd be expecting me,' he said, ignoring her tone, his voice low and silky. 'I know you said you needed to get some sleep but I thought—'

'Well, you thought wrong,' she said, instantly guilty as

she caught his frown so that, to make it up to him, she drew him close. 'Sorry. I really am exhausted, darling, and I need my sleep.'

'Okay. I understand but you owe me one.' Accepting the inevitable, he kissed her gently. 'Sleep all you like but I'm staying here with you.'

'Thanks.' The soft touch of his lips with no passion attached meant a lot, that and the gentlemanly way he accepted the rebuff. He could be so very nice.

And she really was sleepy.

But now of course, perversely, within minutes she was wide awake even as she heard his breathing quieten as he in turn began to drift off.

'What do you make of my family?' she asked, nudging him awake.

The room was too hot, stuffy, and it was too quiet, a quiet she had once known and loved. The flat she lived in now was on a busy road and all night long there was the constant hum of traffic, cars changing gear just outside her window and accelerating up the hill. She often wondered what on earth people were doing driving around at night, for it never eased up until shortly before dawn when there was a lull. Never a night owl, she often woke shortly after dawn and the silence then was blissful, a time for slowly coming out of her sleep knowing that she needn't get up quite yet. That early-morning half-awake state was the best time of day for her, the time when she did her thinking, the time when many of her work ideas came to her. She had no need to bother with an alarm clock, much preferring her own gentle wake-up call and once out of bed she wasted no time in having her first shot of caffeine and a brisk shower. On most working days she could be dressed and out of the flat in twenty minutes.

'What do I make of your family?' Brian echoed her words, moving to lie on his back, taking more than half the duvet with him. 'I don't know. They seem a mixed bunch. Monique doesn't fit in with the rest of you.'

She had not bothered to draw the curtains but it was dark still and she reached out to switch on one of the bedside lamps, which sent out a soft rosy glow. She propped herself up so that she could see him better. 'Happy Christmas,' she said softly. 'In what way doesn't she fit in?'

Brian had the most extraordinary hazel eyes that seemed to have the ability to change colour and she wondered if he was short-sighted because sometimes he narrowed them as if he was finding it difficult to see. There was no evidence of glasses or contacts but then she imagined he would be far too vain to admit to short-sightedness, which he would see as a weakness.

'She's so unlike you all,' he laughed quietly. 'She looks like a little doll who's been dressed in the wrong clothes by an excited little girl.'

'She has her own style,' she said, peculiarly defensive on Monique's behalf. 'And of course she doesn't look like us because she's not blood related.'

'It's not just that. Does she get on with your father?'

'She doesn't work hard enough for his liking. He doesn't think being an artist is much of a job.'

'He's wrong. It's a very special job but I can see that he's a pragmatic sort of guy who would think that. Is she as talented as her husband thinks?'

'I'm the wrong person to ask. I'm afraid I'm biased. I agree with Dad that she should be out there earning her share.'

'She's a homemaker she tells me.'

'Well, yes and if she had kids then I could just about understand it. It must be hell combining work with kids, which is why I'm not going down that road. But Monique doesn't have kids, does she? Unless … ' she glanced at him. 'Is she pregnant?'

'How the hell would I know?'

'I thought she might have told you. You seemed to be

getting on very well together.'

'Surely you don't think I'm interested in her?'

'Of course not.' She laughed that off but it made her feel uncomfortable because he had certainly been guilty of ignoring her rather obviously last night whilst cosying up with Monique. 'The truth is I'm still struggling to get on with her and if that's bitchy then I'm sorry. I suppose I should make more of an effort for Mike's sake. Oh God, it's hellishly hot in here. Do you mind if I turn off the radiator?'

'Be my guest.'

Just for a moment as she slipped barefoot across the room the thought of making love crossed her mind, for it would take nothing to persuade him, but even as she considered it she saw that Brian had swung out of bed in turn and was reaching for the bathrobe her mum had provided.

Bemused, she thought that they were acting like an old married couple, when waking up and not being able to get back off to sleep meant just one thing: a cup of tea. It was rather fun, creeping around in the kitchen in the middle of the night, shushing theatrically so as not to wake her mother and father and afterwards as they sat at the kitchen table mugs clasped in their hands, Amy reflected that this was, in fact, all right, that she was being much too picky and that, for all his faults, she did love him in a fashion and she should simply relax and let things take their course.

There was no harm in allowing herself to think of the future and she did always like to plan ahead.

It was too soon yet but if at some stage Brian did decide to propose she might very well take him up on it.

Chapter Eight

The snow was a satisfactory depth by the following morning and the garden looked wonderful, perfect for Christmas Day. Leaning on the bedroom window sill Christine sighed with pleasure. So far so good.

The meal last night had gone well, the handing over of presents equally well, with a few surprises at that. Conversation had stayed clear of controversial matters although because of that Brian had not opened up as much as she would have liked. She needed to orchestrate a situation where there was just the two of them but that would not be easy. She had suggested a board game after dinner, a Christmas Eve tradition, but to her disappointment the general consensus was that it would go on forever and they were all pleasantly stuffed and just wanted to sit it out. Perhaps it was just as well as it brought out the worst of the competitive edge of both Frank and Amy and usually ended, if not in tears, in irritation.

With a nod towards Monique who strongly opposed television they sat and chatted instead, batting the conversation back and forth. Because Brian, a stranger, was in their midst they kept it general and the business was not mentioned. Frank and Amy disappeared for a while, locked in the family room, and she did not disturb them, for it was always good for the two of them to talk. In an odd way she was jealous of the easy relationship they enjoyed; Amy was very much a daddy's girl. It was always daddy whom the little Amy ran to, daddy who had scooped her up in his arms, daddy who had wished her well when she made the decision to let them down whilst she had been blisteringly angry at what she felt was a betrayal of the very highest order. Frank was a different person round Amy and she knew he missed her being here at home with them more than she did.

The two of them seemed cheerful enough when they came back into the room with Amy going to sit beside Brian who was in the middle of an animated discussion about art with Monique. She wished Amy would not make it quite so obvious that she disliked her sister-in-law although dislike was perhaps too strong a word; Monique was just too far away from Amy on the personality shelf and nothing would ever change that.

After Mike and Monique had gone home, setting out in that splendid magical white night-light that comes with snow, she returned to the sitting room resigned to spending some time alone with Amy and Brian even though she was by now very tired. However, Mike and Monique's departure had been the signal for a general dispersal with Frank, rather sweetly, providing everybody with a bedtime hot chocolate, so any further conversation was curtailed.

Just like the smallest child on this special night, she slept fitfully, hearing Amy moving around downstairs and the murmur of voices sometime around two o'clock but wisely deciding not to investigate further.

'What do you think of him?' she asked Frank now, glancing at her watch, for if everything was to be ready in time for Christmas lunch she had to keep to the schedule pinned on the kitchen notice board.

'Not sure,' he said, sitting up in bed, fussing with pillows and so on before turning his attention back to her. 'Can you believe this? He says he never gives tips. He doesn't believe in them, apparently. I ask you. Where would our lads be without their tips?'

'That's not the end of the world. I sometimes think we're far too quick to give them and being careful with money is no bad thing. In fact it's to be recommended.'

'He drives a brand new Merc.'

'Good for him. So he can keep Amy in the way she is accustomed?' she said tartly. 'You needn't worry about that. I don't believe it's serious for a minute.'

'That's what she says. What do *you* make of him?'

Going to sit on the bed, still in her dressing gown, she pondered the question.

'I'm not that keen,' she admitted at last. 'Can't put my finger on it but I don't think he's the man for her. They don't look comfortable together, not in the way that Mike and Monique do or you and me for that matter,' she added as an afterthought but not before she caught his amused look. 'I know she says she's never getting married but a woman can suddenly change her mind. I do hope she's not getting desperate, clutching at straws because at her age there aren't a lot of men available, not without a load of baggage, anyway. I don't even know if he's been married before or if there are children in the equation. Has she asked him? He seems to keep everything very close to his chest. I'll try and wheedle something out of him.'

'I wouldn't bother. He'll be out of her life soon, I think I can guarantee that. Don't spoil today.'

She had no intention of spoiling the day although as it turned out Frank himself would spoil it big time.

If Christine had half expected an announcement of the impending baby sometime during the day it never happened. The other announcement when it came was totally unexpected. Over Christmas lunch they wore the silly hats, Brian entering into the spirit of things as they laughed over the awful cracker jokes. It was another family tradition that she bought the cheapest Christmas crackers she could find just for the sheer joy of tipping out the contents and seeing whose was the most ridiculous.

As they relaxed over coffee and mince pies, she saw Monique and Mike exchange a glance and her heart lifted for she had anticipated this and thought she knew what was coming. She was very nearly ready to get out the champagne glasses but stopped dead as Mike gave a little cough and spoke. She knew immediately from his expression that whatever it was there was not a baby in the offing.

'We have something to tell you,' he said sharing a quick glance with Monique. 'Haven't we, darling?'

'What?' A silence had fallen and it was a full minute – a long minute's silence – before Mike spoke again.

'I'm sorry, Mum, but we have to tell you something that we know you're not going to like but we do hope you're going to be happy for us and as for you, Dad …' he looked at his father, who looked every bit as puzzled as Christine. 'Well, it's going to be a big shock and I'm sorry for that but it's something we've thought about very seriously and it's something we want to try. We have this fantastic opportunity and we can't let it slip.'

'Opportunity?' Her mouth felt dry and for a moment she felt annoyed with Mike for breaking private family news when a stranger was present, for she was not sure what her reaction would be. If things became strained, if an argument erupted, then the last thing she wanted was for Brian to witness it. He was not part of this family and she suspected and hoped he never would be. 'What sort of opportunity?' she continued, aware her voice had cooled. She felt chilly, in fact, because her Christmas dress was not very warm and wearing a cardigan or shrug over it. even a lovely cashmere one would ruin the effect. Now, as they all fell silent, she could not imagine what he was about to say and wanted to urge him to spit it out, whatever it was, and not keep them in suspense a moment longer.

'We've had a bit of luck. Monique's Aunt Sylvie has given

us this cottage in France,' he said, taking a deep breath and allowing it to sink in. 'Monique's mother inherited it way back but never lived there and now she's left it to Sylvie in her will but Sylvie wants *us* to have it.'

'France?' She glanced at Frank for support as she tried to grasp it. 'Whereabouts in France?'

'It's in Normandy.' Monique explained with a nervous smile, reaching for her husband's hand. 'It's near Honfleur. Do you know Honfleur? It will be fantastic for my painting,' she went on, eyes shining. 'Did you know that there is a special light like there is in St Ives? It will be such an inspiration for me.'

'I've heard that artists love it there,' Brian butted in.

'Exactly.' She looked at him gratefully. 'I might even carry on with the landscapes and seascapes. I can set up by the harbour there and—'

'Hang on a minute. Has your mother died?' Christine interrupted, waiting for the imperceptible nod. 'For goodness' sake, Monique, you might have told me.'

'She didn't want to tell anybody,' Mike said. 'It was her way of dealing with it, Mum.'

'I could have helped,' she said deeply hurt that Monique had felt unable to confide in her. For heaven's sake what hadn't she done to help this girl? She dreaded to think what the little hand-outs amounted to over the years – it wasn't something she had discussed with Frank. It was a little mother/daughter thing except that she had never ever given Amy, her real daughter, any financial help whatsoever.

Monique looked especially lovely today; for a change there was colour in her cheeks and her hair was pulled back into a high swinging ponytail. 'It's not going to be so difficult to get there. You can get the ferry over to one of the Channel ports or you could use the tunnel and drive down. I've got a picture of the cottage in my bag.'

'I don't want to see a picture of it,' Christine could not

stop the childish remark and instantly regretted it. Amy, however, reached over and took the photograph from Monique saying nothing but handing it over immediately for Brian to look at. From their expressions it would seem that they were impressed by what they saw.

'Are you telling us that you are moving there?' Christine was trying to keep her voice steady. 'Is that it?'

'Well, yes, of course we are when we can get things organized.' Mike said, watching them all carefully, his manner strangely defiant.

'So you'll be handing in your notice?' Frank's voice was nowhere near as firm as usual and she was furious suddenly, for in his condition he shouldn't be dealt shocks like this. 'This is all very sudden. You might have informed me earlier, Mike.'

'I'm informing you now, Dad.' Mike's voice was low and determined. 'I will, of course, not leave immediately. I intend to work out a proper notice,' he added stiffly. 'And don't pretend it's going to matter either way. You know I've never liked the job. You've never thought me up to it.'

There was a sharp intake of breath from Frank. 'That's not true,' he said firing a quick glance at Christine.

'What will you do there?' she asked her son, choosing not to look at Monique. 'It might sound wonderful like some extended holiday but it's not very practical, is it? You'll have to earn a living somehow.'

'Exactly. You might not have much money coming in from Monique's paintings,' Frank said. It was a statement of fact and he was being remarkably calm even though Christine knew he had been dealt a serious below-the-belt blow.

'Aunt Sylvie has found Mike a job already in one of her ex-husband's restaurants,' Monique said, eyes flashing as she glanced sharply at her father-in-law. 'She's on good terms with both her exes.'

'Good for her.' Amy seemed amused by all this, returning the photograph to Monique.

'But Mike doesn't speak French? Neither of you speaks French,' Christine said helplessly, clutching at straws to find a negative in all this.

'We'll soon pick it up and they all speak English anyway,' Monique said with a Gallic shrug, practising, no doubt, for when she was back in her native country.

'That's lucky,' Christine said, sarcasm to the fore. 'But if I were you I wouldn't be in a rush to sell your house until you see if it works out.'

It sounded a half-baked idea to her and she suddenly resented this marvellous-sounding Aunt Sylvie, who seemed to have it all worked out.

'We're not fools. We've thought about this a lot.' Monique was defensive, looking at Mike for support. 'Aunt Sylvie feels guilty that my mother left me nothing and she is more than happy to help us out financially until we can get things sorted out. She's done very well out of her marriages. She was married to Henri-Jacques Gaillon, you know.'

None of them had heard of him but it turned out he was a renowned chef specializing in fish dishes and with more than enough restaurants scattered around the Normandy and Brittany coasts.

You could cut the atmosphere now with a knife and Christine could not think of anything to say. The most glaring thing uppermost in her mind was the ungratefulness of it all and now that Monique had somebody else to fund her expensive tastes she was no longer needed. She was annoyed with herself for feeling this way, for she had never once begrudged any of the money or gifts she had given her daughter-in-law but it felt, rightly or wrongly, that she was being kicked in the teeth for her generosity.

First and foremost, though, she was a good hostess and drawing on all her reserves she pulled herself together. She would get through this gracefully if it killed her.

'Congratulations!' she said, hearing her voice from afar.

'Absolutely. Well done, you two. How wonderful to be

given a cottage in France,' Amy said, shooting a warning glance at her mother before getting up and spinning round to look at them all. 'Isn't that fabulous news? I wish you all the best with it and I'll be the first to visit. Let's drink a toast.'

'Thank you, Amy.' Monique smiled uncertainly. 'We would love to have you visit, when we get things sorted a bit, of course. We have to find it first of all. My aunt hasn't seen it for years either but it's being looked after for her.'

Christine dare not look at Frank.

'Yes, let's drink a toast,' she said. Her world had just fallen to pieces, the vision of her little baby grandchild disappearing fast but she was determined to see it through with some grace. It was Christmas Day for heaven's sake and she was not going to allow this to spoil it. 'I'll fetch another bottle of wine.'

'Make it champagne,' Frank said, recovering, too. 'It's not every day we get news like this.'

Chapter Nine

Christine needed to get out of the house. Trying to keep calm, trying to take it in, she suggested a walk through the village and up the hill. She was trying her best to be sensible and to understand that the move to France to live in the cottage Monique had been gifted could only be good news for the young couple. They would put the house on River Terrace up for sale and provided they could sell in today's tough market they might make a small profit from that. As for Mike, she wondered how he would cope in a country where he couldn't speak the language but he seemed excited by the prospect and it would give him the chance to show his father that he was capable of doing something with his life. Mike was not the impulsive type, though, and she wondered how much this whole thing was being driven by Monique. She was beginning to realize that there might be more to Monique than the shy, butter-wouldn't-melt look suggested.

Although she wanted to exit the room and be on her own a while once the news was out, she had no choice with Brian being present but to stay put and look as if she was pleased. She finally relented and asked to see the photograph of the cottage. It looked lovely with its half-timbered façade. It had a brown-tiled roof and reminded her of a gingerbread house sitting there in a pretty little garden full of flowers with a wooden gate and a narrow path leading to the door and the shuttered windows. This whole concept was a touch too fairy tale-like for her but trying to make sense of it she realized that if she and Frank had been given a similar opportunity when they were young they would surely have jumped at it. Although, on second thoughts, would Frank ever have dared walk away from the business?

Oh goodness, it was all much too complicated. It was Christmas Day and she was in no mood for this. With a smile, she excused herself for a moment and swiftly went upstairs to her room, sat down on the bed and tried to compose herself. She felt close to tears but that would help nobody. With a supreme effort she pulled herself together and changed out of her dress into something more casual before returning to the fray.

'Let's have a walk. Who's coming with me?'

'A walk?' Frank looked at her as if she had suggested they take a trip to the moon. They used to take long walks once upon a time but lately they never seemed to fit them in, even though he was supposed to take regular and frequent exercise.

'I'll come with you, Mum,' Mike said, looking relieved at the way she had taken the news, unable to see through the part she was playing of the delighted-for-you mother and imagine for one second that she might not be genuinely thrilled about it all.

'I'll come, too,' Amy said, smiling sympathetically and for her part seeing through her completely.

'Oh, all right then, I can see I'm outnumbered,' Frank said, cheerfully enough. 'I'm in.'

'Would you mind if I didn't join you?' Brian, who had sat quietly through the family drama, spoke up now. 'I need to make a few phone calls and use my lap-top.'

'Not business, surely?' Christine said for Amy had told her he had no family to speak of so who could he be ringing?

'I'm afraid so,' he said with an apologetic grimace.

'I think I'll stay put too.' Monique had excelled herself today, dressed in festive scarlet like Christine although

Monique's ankle-length velour concoction was much more striking. 'I just want to curl up here.'

Here was the large comfortable sofa in front of the log fire and indeed it was tempting just to sit in the warm and guzzle chocolates and nuts but Christine knew she would feel heaps better and invigorated if she had a brisk walk.

Getting everybody organized and into suitable attire for the trip outdoors was every bit as bad as it used to be when they were kids but at last they were ready, just the four of them, Frank surprisingly upbeat as they set out. It felt like old times especially as they would be doing the very same walk they had done for years when the children were small. The children had grumbled then about going out for a walk on Christmas Day afternoon unless there was a dolly's pram or a new bike to try out. Seeing her grown-up children setting out ahead of them, Christine sighed, the memory of earlier happier times hitting her hard.

'Bit of a facer, all this,' Frank said, taking her gloved hand and giving it a squeeze. 'Are you all right?'

'Not really,' she sighed, though pleased at the unexpected concern. 'It wasn't quite what I was expecting.'

'It's saved me a lot of bother,' he went on. 'Having him resign means I don't have to ask him to leave. And say what you will, Christine, we were going to have to face up to that sooner or later before he buggered things up completely.'

'You've never given him a chance.'

'Oh come on, I've given him every chance. He's just not up to it.'

'We can't force either of them to go into the business if they don't want to. And I wouldn't want to lumber either of them just now with something that's going to fail.'

'It is not going to fail. What put that idea into your head? We've got a good little business going. It's not like you to be pessimistic.' His exasperation spilled over and he let go of her hand abruptly. 'We will get through it. It's just a blip.'

She was not going to spoil it by reminding him that she had put a hefty chunk of cash into the business recently to tide them over and that this was potentially much more than a blip unless they did something drastic. There were many more removal firms these days in this area so they had to be competitive. They needed to drum up trade but the next few months were the quiet months in the domestic market so it was going to be extra hard. There was no point in worrying him more than he was already but even as she tried to think of some encouraging words he forged ahead to catch up with the children. As he moved forward Amy dropped back and waited for her to catch up.

'Let the men have a chat,' she said, smiling. 'I don't think they get much of a chance outside the office to talk about stuff. Mike's just been telling me how he has agonized about things but he has to think of Monique first. She's going to be sorry to move and she hates to leave you but they would be daft not to go.'

'I know that.' Christine waved a hand in frustration.

'He's been telling me about his new job. It's not just a restaurant, apparently; there is a hotel attached and Mike's going to be helping to run that.'

'Good heavens, he has no experience whatsoever. How the hell is that going to work?'

'Give him a chance.' Amy tugged at her fluffy cream beret. It had been a so-called stocking present together with some matching mittens and scarf and she was gamely wearing the whole caboodle, although Christine suspected she might never wear them again. She looked pretty today, even happy, and Christine wondered what had gone on last night in the kitchen.'We've given him enough chances,' she said, trying to keep the bitterness out of her voice and not quite succeeding. 'And I've had to fight him every inch of the way to stop him losing patience.'

'It might be the making of him, Mum. He was never interested in our business.'

'I don't want to talk about it any more just now.'

The snow was soft underfoot with occasional slippery patches and they took care, she and Amy allowing some distance to develop between them and the men. Frank seemed to be taking it better than she was and she needed to give him time to talk to his son in a sensible manner. Perhaps it *would* be the best thing for Mike, an opportunity indeed to prove to his father that he was capable of making a success of something on his own. Even so, the news lay like a solid block of ice in her stomach and just now she did not feel capable of ever eating again. Pity, because she had a big buffet lined up for later where the Christmas cake would take centre stage.

There were few people about as most of the villagers were huddled indoors but it felt good, the familiarity a comfort as they trudged through the village street, over the stone bridge then over the stile that would take them along the narrow public footpath up to the top of the hill. There was usually a wonderful view from up there and today it would be exceptional. They would need to get the walk over quite quickly, though, before the daylight dwindled. Hot toddies when they got back, she thought, and she hoped to goodness that Monique and Brian had kept the fire topped up. She was just a little concerned at leaving the two of them together because, although she trusted Monique completely she was not so sure of Brian. He had a robust earthy look about him and looking back she supposed that when he was young Frank's demeanour had been similar.

'Brian should have come along,' she said, deciding, on reflection, that in fact it was better he had not because she must grasp this heaven-sent opportunity for a mother/daughter chat.

'He's not into country walks,' Amy said.

'But he lives in the country, doesn't he?'

'Yes but he's only fifteen minutes away from civilization. I think he'll sell up before long and move back to the city.

He misses that buzz.'

'From what he says it's much too big for him, anyway. Unless he's intending to get married and start a family and wanted a house ready made for them.' She shot Amy a quick glance. 'Is it serious between the two of you?'

Amy sighed. 'I don't think so.'

'You don't *think* so? Don't you know?'

'How sure were you when Dad asked you to marry him? Did you say yes straight off?'

'No,' she admitted. 'I made him wait a while. Your grandma and grandpa didn't really like him that much and that didn't help. You always want other people to like the man you choose, don't you? Has he asked you to marry him?'

'Not yet but I think he might.'

'I see. And will you say yes?'

'You don't like him, do you?'

'Oh come on, we've only just met him.' Christine sighed and tucked her arm into Amy's. 'It's up to you, love, and we won't interfere. If he's what you want then that's fine with us but can I offer you some advice?'

Amy smiled a little. 'You're going to whether I like it or not.'

'Yes, well, don't dawdle too much. It's so easy to talk yourself out of something, something that might be right for you. Just think about that.'

'Thanks. At least you haven't said that I'm not getting any younger and no, Mum, I'm not desperate yet. I can still have children if I want. I'm not shutting that door completely.'

Christine glanced at her in surprise. That was the very first time she had said anything like that, a little softening in that tough-nut exterior, and she welcomed it cautiously. Who knows? She would grow used to Brian in time and that might be enough. It was a crumb of comfort, anyway.

Frank and Mike had picked up the pace and were forging

ahead. At least they were talking, which was something. Amy noticed it, too, and pointed it out.

'This is the best thing to happen, Mum. It was a big mistake the two of them working together,' she said. 'That's why I turned down the chance because I just knew it wouldn't work out. Dad would never treat me as an equal because I'm still his little girl and to the staff I would always be the boss's daughter who didn't quite deserve the job. It's not many families that can work together without a few big bust ups and it might have been better if Mike had stuck up for himself a bit more.'

'Of course it would but he's not like that. He's not as argumentative as you, not by a long chalk.'

'Arguments are good. They can be positive and they clear the air. If you don't have it out then it all festers and that's no good for anybody. Do you and Dad argue much?'

'No. You know we don't. I sulk and that's much more effective,' she said with a small smile.

At this point the path narrowed even more and forked to the right. It was the hardest part of the whole climb, which on the whole was gentle enough. The hill the village clustered beneath was an easily accessible affair, child's play for anybody of average fitness. The snow was making the path slippery, though, and even with suitable footwear it was tiring trudging through it.

'We don't need to do the whole hog,' Christine said. 'We can turn back anytime you like.'

'No fear. I haven't reached the summit for a long time.'

'The summit? It's hardly Everest.'

'It feels like it when you're not fit.' She paused, hands on hips. 'Good grief, Mum, I'm knackered already.'

'The gym membership Brian gave you should help.'

'It would if I meant to use it. When have I the time to go to the gym?'

'You should make the time, darling.'

'It's easier said than done, Mum. And I'm just a bit miffed

that he thinks I need to get fit. I *do* need to get fitter but he needn't have reminded me.' She changed the subject abruptly as she caught her mother's smile. 'Dad seems to be recovering well. What does the doctor say?'

'Providing he keeps up the medication, watches his blood pressure and stops smoking he should be fine.' Christine sighed, pausing briefly to catch her own breath and taking a moment to gaze back at the snowy landscape. 'It was very scary, Amy, especially with the family history. He was checked years ago and all seemed well but he ducked out of future checks, which was ridiculous because they might have picked up a problem. Do you mind if we don't talk about it? It upsets me.'

Amy nodded, understanding. 'It upsets me too, Mum. But the operation was a success, wasn't it?'

'Oh yes. Provided he does what he's told he's good to go, the doctor says, for another twenty years or so.' Christine managed a smile. 'So you needn't worry because we're stuck with him a while longer.'

'I'm sorry you had to cope with it on your own, Mum. I would have stayed a while longer when he came out of hospital but I was so busy.'

'I know. Monique was here. She was such a help.'

'I'm sure she was.' The tone had cooled but that always happened when Monique was mentioned. 'You're going to miss her.'

'Yes.'

'You can visit. She's quite right. It's not that far.'

'Don't humour me, Amy. It takes me five minutes just now to get to her house and it will take at least two days to get to the one in France,' Christine said and that put an end to that. 'If she does have a child I'm going to miss it growing up. And it will be French.'

Amy laughed. 'So? I think that's rather sweet.'

'Yes, of course it is. Tell me I'm being daft.'

'You are not being daft. You are just upset, that's all. As

for her having a baby, I don't think she's keen on that idea, Mum. If she was then she'd have had one by now.'

'Do you think so?' Christine asked wistfully, knowing she was right.

They were past the worst bit of the climb now as the path levelled out and they paused to take in the view of the village in the distance. Smoke from chimneys below billowed to join the fluff of the clouds and it looked very much as if there might be more snow.

'I think your dad's still smoking on the sly but what can I do about it?' Christine said. 'It really is up to him. Would you have a word? He might take some notice of you.'

'I'll try but in the end he'll do what he wants.'

They were interrupted by a shout from above them. Momentarily, Frank and Mike were out of view but suddenly Mike appeared running and skidding down the slope.

'It's Dad,' he cried as he neared them. 'We have to get help. He's collapsed.'

Amy whipped her mobile out. 'Do we need an ambulance?'

'Of course we need a bloody ambulance.'

'Fuck. There's no signal … can you get one on yours?'

'Shit, no.'

Ignoring her children's appalling language, Christine was already rushing along the path to where Frank was now sitting on the frozen ground. Her first thought was a ridiculous one; he was wearing the brand new overcoat she had bought him which would be ruined.

He was breathing and trying to smile. Together, somehow, they got him to his feet and managed to get him to a conveniently placed bench, a bench with a little plaque on it in memory of a local man who apparently often sat at this spot to study the view. There was a faint dusting of snow on the bench and Christine brushed at it with her glove before sitting down beside him.

'What is it, Mum?' Amy asked anxiously.

'Don't panic,' she said, seeing the fear in her daughter's eyes. 'He'll be fine.'

But, as she caught his gasp, the ashen face, the look in his eyes, she knew in her heart that this time he would not.

'Hang on, Dad,' Amy was saying soothingly. 'They'll be here soon.'

Helplessly, Christine looked round at the silent scene before them. She could see Mike who had hared along and was very nearly back at the stile. The phone call for help would be made in minutes. Amy was squeezed on the bench now on the other side of her father, holding his hand and offering consoling words. Sitting there looking up at the sky as the first flurry of a fresh snowfall drifted down, Christine's anxiety was replaced by a sudden ridiculous and totally unfounded exasperation.

'Oh for God's sake, it's so typical of him,' she wailed, stamping her cold feet in the boots and slapping her gloved hands together in a vain attempt to find some warmth. 'Would you believe it, today of all days?'

PART TWO

Chapter Ten

Today, for the first time this year there was some warmth in the air. Birdsong accompanied the traffic noise this morning, a perky happy sound that surely heralded the onset of spring.

Amy chose to walk through the little park to the bus stop just for the joy of it. As parks go it wasn't great but the spring flowers, bless them, were not allowing the slightly grim surroundings to disturb them. They were out in abundance, a riot of blues and yellows, and her pace quickened as she headed along the path. She was wearing her work heels and making a clicking sound as she walked thinking that now that spring was approaching she needed to get some new clothes; a couple of lighter-weight suits and some paler tights, for she considered it unprofessional to go bare-legged to the office, but nor did she feel entirely comfortable wearing trousers for work. Spring brought out the best and the worst of the English and she had just caught a glimpse of the worst; a middle-aged man wearing a vest, shorts, black socks and sandals, his legs painfully pale. She could not avoid a passing horrified glance at him.

'Good morning.' A woman smiled at her in passing but then morning sunshine and the promise of a lovely day did that to people. It made them aware of others suddenly in a way that was not always apparent in the depths of winter. What a buttoned-up race we are, she thought, with our heads constantly bowed in the rain and wind. It had turned out to be a warmer than average winter but that had meant rain and dull miserable grey days, clear crisp cold ones in short supply.

Amy had felt guilty that she was not able to spend more time with her mother and with that in mind she had applied for an admin job in a Preston department store and had what she thought was a good second interview. She had not mentioned it yet to her mother because she did not want to get her hopes up.

Christmas Day and the following morning keeping vigil by her father's bedside had been desperately difficult for everybody but somehow they all pulled together and got through it. It killed the romance with Brian, though; just when she had started to have hopes of him, just when she had started to envisage a lifetime together, just when she had started to dare to make plans and more importantly just when she needed him the most, he let her down. It often took a crisis for people to reveal their true selves, although her own take on it had been to lose all semblance of the business-like exterior she normally presented to the world and in its place she became a blubbering wreck. Monique, on the contrary, lost her default helpless look and became a surprising tower of strength. In fact, just briefly, as Monique offered her a comforting little cuddle she felt a surprising affection towards her that she had never before experienced.

'Sorry, I can't cope with all this,' Brian had said as they walked down the hospital corridor late on Christmas Day. Her father, his condition having worsened, had been moved to a small high-intensity ward hooked up to machines whilst the doctors did their bit. Her mother was being looked after by Mike and Monique and Amy had felt the desperate need to escape for a while. Christmas or no Christmas, life and sometimes death went along just the same in this place.

There was a brightly decorated Christmas tree by the café and a surprising number of people milling around but as had just been proved, illness makes no allowance for special dates.

Her father had been brought in by ambulance and they had followed by car, hanging round for ages whilst he was processed and eventually being allowed up to the ward on the seventh floor.

'Oh look, he's got a lovely view,' her mother said and they all nodded in agreement. The shock seemed to have deprived them of sensible conversation and on the journey in through treacherous roads covered in slushy snow they had talked a load of utter nonsense, none of which she could remember. Her father was now lying there quietly. On the way to hospital something had left him and Amy could not put her finger on what – it might have been hope. She was glad to escape the vigil for a while and in any case there were too many of them to sit round the bed; a nurse had kindly but firmly indicated as much.

'I'm not good with hospitals,' Brian went on, looking pale himself although she could only hazard a guess as to how she herself looked.

'Neither am I,' she said, the question answered as she caught a glimpse of herself in the hospital shop window. She looked a fright. Mike had rallied around and taken charge, dealing with everything, liaising with the medical staff and passing on the news gently to them in a way that surprised her. The doctor, a very nice woman, had instinctively looked to him, which at any other time would have irritated the pants off her.

Mike was her brother and as she had explained to Brian they hadn't always got on but just now, as with Monique, she felt an overwhelming fondness for him, a sisterly love that comforted her. She tried to tell him that but was too embarrassed to say it. It was not enough, though, for she needed the support of Brian, too. She was scared, afraid that her father was not going to make it and she needed this man beside her but she knew from his expression that he was going to desert her. It was just a question of when and she could not believe that he would be so crass as to do it now.

'Cup of coffee or tea?' he suggested nudging her towards the café. 'You should eat something.'

She felt guilty at leaving her mother even if it was only for fifteen minutes but she needed the break and she sat down on an orange plastic chair as he went to get the coffee.

He came back with that and two mince pies. The coffee was scalding hot and the mince pies were cold, dusted with icing sugar.

'Didn't they offer to warm them up?' she asked, a ridiculous question, for what the hell did it matter. They were inedible in any case but just now she would have been hard pressed to eat one of her mother's delicious home-made ones. Her Christmas dinner was still sitting heavily in her stomach so, ignoring the mince pie, she took a tentative sip of the coffee.

'I have things to do,' Brian said, sipping his own and not even looking properly at her. He was wearing the sweater she had bought him, his leather jacket discarded over the back of the chair and she had a sudden desperate need to cuddle up to him, to be held firmly in his arms, to be told, true or not, that everything was going to be just fine. 'If you don't mind I'll get myself back home. I feel a bit in the way here as if I'm intruding.'

He had no car but she did not bother to ask how he was going to get back.

'Suit yourself,' she said. 'But if you walk out now you can forget about us.'

'Oh come on, darling. It was just a bit of fun between us, you said that yourself,' he said, his casual tone and his lack of respect for the situation infuriating her. 'It's not as if we are engaged or anything. In any case I'm in no position to get married.'

'Who said anything about getting married? I thought I made that quite clear when we started out.'

'The ladies have been known to change their minds,' he said. 'And you can't deny that your mother's been looking at me and sizing me up as a potential husband for you.'

'She has not,' she retorted and it was true because her mother had behaved remarkably well as far as that was concerned although she had no doubt been pinning her hopes on a tête-à-tête with Brian at some stage. 'Why are you in no position to get married? Are you married already?' she asked, finding herself not entirely surprised when he gave a small nod.

'The divorce is going through.'

'Children?' she inquired briskly.

'Two. Boy and girl.'

'You bastard.'

A woman at another table glanced their way quickly, looking away again as she caught Amy's eye.

She felt the tears she had been doing her best to hold back welling up; after all, she had cared about this man, in a way, although thinking back she had always been half-hearted about the relationship, so maybe it served her right. She had been trying to persuade herself, she realized, that this was it, that he would be as good a bet as anybody else and my God, wasn't she being given a much needed escape route?

'Look, I'm sorry,' he went on. 'This is bloody awful. I was going to tell you after Christmas just in case you'd got it into your head that it was serious between us and then all this stuff happened.'

'All this stuff?' she echoed, voice rising. 'For heaven's sake, Brian, my father is dying.'

'No he's not. He'll recover, you'll see. They can do wonders with drugs and therapy and the like. Heart problems are not what they used to be.'

'And since when have you been an expert?' She shook her head, watching a group of people flooding through the entrance door looking very worried. She heard one of them ask for A&E and thought to herself that there was another family whose Christmas had been cocked up, not just now but forever.

'I'm no expert and I'm only trying to cheer you up,' he said and she gave an apologetic nod. 'I'm sorry, Amy, but I can't take on any more problems. I have enough of my own. My wife's being difficult. She's trying to take me for all she can get.'

'Well, forgive me for not caring. You might have told me about the children.'

'I was going to.' His expression was fleetingly shamefaced and just for the merest second she felt a little sorry for him but that quickly slipped by. She had been a fool and warning bells should have sounded when he was so cagey about his private life. She had, she saw, just been a convenient lay for him. He had probably seen her as a single woman desperate for sex and that thought depressed her, for hadn't she used him, too? For the last five years she had been the one on her own at Christmas; Mum and Dad, Mike and Monique and her; five settings at table when six would be a much more comfortable arrangement.

She had brought Brian along simply to show them that she was capable of having a boyfriend, partner, whatever, that she was not all business.

'No hard feelings?' He was anxious to leave and she remembered now that, during their frantic dash to the hospital she had thought it strange that he had turned up with his bag packed. He picked up that bag now and shrugged himself into the jacket. 'Look, I hope it works out. I hope he's okay.'

'Just go,' she told him wearily.

And he did just that.

He did not even look back.

And it was the following day, at lunchtime, that her father lost his fight for life.

Daniel understood when she phoned to tell him the news, telling her to take as much time off as she needed to. The Christmas panic was over and he and Janet would cope with whatever the New Year sales had to throw at them. It was almost too late anyway; they could do nothing more, for the Christmas figures were already written in stone.

In the event she got herself back to work as soon as possible following the funeral. Her mother had insisted and although it was a bit of a trek she did the journey back home every weekend in the early days until she felt her mother was recovering from what had been a terrible shock. On her first day back, Janet hugged her, tears in her eyes, asking if she was quite sure she was ready to come back. Daniel, more reserved, had simply nodded his sympathy and said it was good to see her.

Now, three months on, things were moving and Daniel was leaving that afternoon. He had requested a low-key goodbye but he wasn't getting away with that; there was to be a buffet in the boardroom for senior members of staff, most of whom would be glad to see the back of him. He had done exactly what had been asked of him and given the store a fighting chance. The Christmas figures had been analyzed and the downward trend had levelled out, which, considering the economic reality, was very satisfactory indeed.

Daniel was not taking up any of the job offers that had come his way. He was taking a risk, perhaps, in setting up his own retail consultancy business but he liked the idea of the freedom that would come with it. He could set up base wherever he liked. Amy was pleased for him, wished him well, of course, but it did leave her in a predicament if the Preston job failed to materialize. She was assured by Mr Armitage that there was a job for her in the Leeds store but it would be a sideways move not a promotion as such and, worse, other people would see it as a demotion and she would be in danger of losing any respect she might have gained. Also, there was still a dribble of resentment at who she was and what she had done because in the initial stages of Daniel's assessment and restructuring a few jobs had, of necessity, been lost.

Coming on top of all her domestic worries, with her future in doubt it had been a depressing few months, although she could give up the rental on her flat with just a month's notice so she was in a good position to move if she needed to.

She boarded the bus, managing to find a spare seat beside a large lady who was using the seat beside her as a receptacle for a heavily laden Sainsbury's carrier bag. Forced to move it, she gave a tut of exasperation.

'Sorry.' Amy said with a smile that was not acknowledged. Ah well, you couldn't expect the lovely spring morning to have the same effect on everybody. Amy made a gallant attempt to start up a conversation about the weather but it was met with silence during the short trip into the city centre. The lady wanted to get off at the stop before Amy's, which entailed a great deal of fussing about, the lady giving her an annoyed look as she slipped past as if it was her fault.

This had the effect of chipping into her good mood and it was with a slightly heavier heart that she finally made it to the store. There was a buzz about the place now, a renewed sense of achievement and promise, largely due to Daniel, of course, and the optimism he had brought about. The January sales had been a qualified success and the windows were full of their spring designs.

'Good morning.' Janet beamed a welcome. 'Isn't it a lovely day?'

'Lovely,' she echoed, going quickly through to her office because she didn't want to get caught up in yet another post-relationship conversation about Brian. Janet was behaving like a dog with a bone where Brian was concerned. She had given Janet the barest facts and she was up in arms about it. She seemed to be under the impression that Brian had meant more to her than he actually had, managing, astonishingly, to blame him for her father's sudden death and she was treating Amy with such maternal concern that it was becoming suffocating. However you looked at it the brief fling had been a humiliating experience and she was in no mood for repeating it. She had behaved badly; never again would she take such a cavalier attitude to casual sex. Nor could she believe that she had actually come close to convincing herself that he was Mr Right when he had been at best Mr Maybe.

'Coffee, love?' Janet was through to her office even before she had hung up her coat. 'Have you had breakfast or shall I get you a croissant too?'

'Just coffee, thanks,' she answered briskly, wondering how best to tell Janet to stop all this fussing. Once Daniel was gone, Janet's role here was over and although she had been offered another job in the organization she had decided to retire but it seemed to be her last wish that she should help Amy find another man.

As Janet disappeared in search of coffee, she glanced through the half-open door and could see Daniel was already installed in his office, no doubt finishing off packing away his personal effects. She knocked and entered. She was wearing her black suit – again – and realized that although she had not intended it, it might look as if she was still in deep mourning.

'Good morning, Daniel.'

'Good morning. I'm hoping to slip away before lunch-time,' he explained, motioning that she should shut the door. 'I hate a fuss and most of all I hate surprise parties. Are they planning something? You can tell me,' he added with a grin. 'I shan't say who spilled the beans.'

'Well, yes, I'm afraid so.' She looked round at the boxes that were stacked everywhere. 'Can I help?'

He pulled a face. 'It's a mess, isn't it? I've got somebody coming up to help me get these down to the car. Maybe you could just put sticky tape around them so that I don't lose anything on the way.'

'I know all there is to know about packing things,' she said, noting that he had filled the boxes far too full with some heavy books. She was aware that she needed to persuade him to stay for the little buffet and speeches. He was the guest of honour, for goodness' sake and it would be a non-starter without him. Mr Armitage would be saying a few heartfelt words, no doubt, and there would be a round of applause and pats on the back coupled with relief that he was finally off.

'They've got a buffet organized,' she said, removing some books from one of the boxes. 'They're going to be very disappointed if you don't show. You can always slip away early, if you must.'

He did not reply for a moment, sitting at the desk now and taking a sip of what must have been cold coffee. Feeling his eyes on her, she busied herself with the books, uncomfortable at the scrutiny.

'What are your plans, Amy?' he asked at last. 'Are you going to take the job offered here or the one in Preston if you get that?'

'I am not going to stay here,' she told him. 'It's tempting because it's the easiest thing to do but I need to move on. As for the Preston job I don't know if I'll take it or not – if I get offered it, that is,' she said. 'Thanks for the reference, by the way, but when they outlined what the job was it wasn't quite what I was expecting. To be honest I'm not sure if I really want it.'

'Never ever accept a job if you have doubts,' he went on with a smile. 'And never accept a job when you are under stress, either, because your judgement is flawed. I've been watching you closely these last few months and I know it's been hard. It must have been dreadful.'

'You have no idea,' she said, bristling suddenly because he really did not. Nobody did. It had shot the family to pieces, the suddenness of it all, put Mike's move to France on hold, which was not going down well with Monique and although the family business was still running it felt as if it was trundling along in third gear. Decisions had to be made and she was uncomfortably aware that with her mother still in a state of shock it was she and Mike who would have to make them. 'On Christmas Day of all days.' She could hear her voice shaking. 'I know it would be just as bad whenever it happened but somehow coming as it did at Christmas it was ten times worse. I'll never enjoy Christmas again.'

'No, of course you won't. It's rotten happening like that.'

'We'd had a wonderful meal, roast beef....' she realized she was in danger of losing it, rushing on before that happened. 'But with hindsight maybe we shouldn't have started on such a strenuous uphill walk right after lunch. Well, it wasn't right after lunch but it was soon after. My brother had just dropped a bombshell on us about moving to France and I think my mother needed some fresh air. I'm sorry, I shouldn't dump all this on you.' She waved a dismissive hand but she could sense the waves of sympathy coming her way, which was always dangerous in her present frame of mind.

'You can tell me if you like.' His voice was so kind and she did not need that. She felt unwelcome tears stinging her eyes and was suddenly furious with herself. She was starting to ramble and become pathetic and she didn't want him to see her like this. It was getting on for three months now and it was time she got a grip. 'Hey. Come and sit down. I'm sorry. I didn't mean to remind you. You're still upset.'

'Of course I am,' she retaliated with sharpness, blinking

away the hot tears. She thought she had done with the crying but it could still get her from time to time. She alone of all the family understood her father and he in turn understood her; theirs was the special relationship. Never once had he rebuked her for not following him into the business. He simply accepted her need to do something else. And Mike was useless so her father had had an uphill struggle trying to cope with him, which can't have helped his condition. She should have talked to him, made him give up the smoking for one, and told him to take it easy, let Mike take the strain.

If only she had talked to him.

Sitting down on the chair facing Daniel's desk, she took a deep breath and regained control as he busied himself with files so that he might avoid looking at her. He had put his hand lightly on her waist to guide her into the chair and although it was a fleeting touch it had sent a shiver through her. He had never touched her before and it astonished her that the little touch had meant so much. She was still trying to sort through her emotions, which were all over the place just now. Grief, sadness, anger at Brian, guilt because she had brought it all on herself. She was emotionally wrung out and that little gentle touch from Daniel meant so much that for two pins she would have turned and nestled into him and cried into his shoulder. He had a wonderfully reassuring shoulder. Where was this going? They were just work colleagues and she did not fancy him. She had never fancied him. He was out of bounds.

Out of the blue she heard herself give a great shuddering sigh, the prelude to another bout of tears and, horrified at the very idea of breaking down in front of him, she pulled herself together with an enormous effort. She caught his glance and how he quickly looked away, knowing that he had her sussed but was thankfully giving her a moment. Just then, Janet bustled in with her coffee, putting it down on the desk before disappearing but not before she had given her a look of concern.

'I'll come along to the buffet if it will help,' Daniel said at last with a resigned smile as, composure regained, she started to re-pack the boxes. 'But let it be known I'm doing it out of duty, pure and simple. I just hope to God they're not going to make a big thing out of it. It wasn't just down to me, to us; it was a big effort on everyone's part. We all pulled together, the whole damned lot of us.'

'Save the speech for later,' she told him. She could afford to do that now that he was leaving. Show him what she was made of. 'Come on; let's get this out of the way.'

They worked in silence until all the boxes were ready to be collected. The office had a bare look about it now as rooms do when books are removed from shelves and as the sunlight shimmered in it showed up the layer of dust on the newly empty desk top.

More than anything else, that told them that they were done.

Mission accomplished.

'Thanks for all you've done, Amy,' he said as she prepared to leave. 'I wonder if—'

'What?' she turned, her hand on the doorknob.

'Perhaps we might have dinner together this evening, just the two of us. I have a proposition to put to you and it isn't fair to do it until I'm officially done here.'

'All right.' It sounded like business, not a date, but her feminine mind was on instant alert particularly when he mentioned a top-class restaurant. She would have to dig out something respectable for that, business or not, and preferably not black because she was done with mourning. A vision of her wardrobe flared in her head telling her that she had absolutely nothing to wear but there was no way she could find time today to root out a suitable dress and, in any case, she could not face an inquisition from Clare, the personal shopper, who would instantly be on her back if she turned up in Ladieswear in search of a frock.

'I'll pick you up at eight,' he offered totally oblivious to the dilemma he was setting her. 'Perhaps you can ask Janet to book a table for us?'

Oh dear. Janet would put two and two together and make goodness knows what although it was a now well-known fact that Daniel was seeing Bea so this was all perfectly innocent. Even so, the prospect of a meal at a fancy restaurant, just the two of them, could put her in an awkward position. Bea would be at the buffet this afternoon but it might be wise not to mention the dinner date just in case it caused that lovely lady to spit feathers.

Chapter Eleven

The garden at Snape House was coming into its own as the weather warmed up and, having moved the clocks forward the days blessedly lengthened. Christine loved the spring, seeing it as a stirring and optimistic season. Down in the village yesterday she had walked past a field full of newly born lambs and for the first time in a long time she had taken the time to stand and watch their antics. Seeing her standing at the gate, the ewes had become anxious, calling out to their offspring who quickly ran to them. If a lamb mistakenly went to the wrong mother it was sharply shown the door and would stand there looking quite alone, bleating until its own mother called out. Her heart lifted when she saw the two of them reunited, the ewe standing patiently whilst the lamb latched on to her. Observing the little gentle moment between the animals caught at her and she was reminded that, when it came down to it, animals had the whole mother/baby thing sorted. It was a whole different ball game when it came to humans.

She asked herself why she did not feel quite the same about Amy as she did about Mike. She ought not to have favourites but somewhere along the line at quite a young age Amy had become independent from her and pushed her aside in a way that Mike had not. Perhaps she, even more than Frank, had wanted their daughter to join them in the family business and had therefore felt betrayed when she turned it down.

This morning she walked across the newly clipped lawn in bright sunshine, that wonderful spring sunshine with none of the sickly heat of deep summer. On mornings like this, she liked to have her coffee sitting on the bench underneath the Japanese cherry, heavily laden with blossom just now and deliciously scented, closing her eyes to breathe in the silence and the perfume. It was not often that they had the time to sit here together and Frank was always too edgy to sit for long, glancing at his watch saying he had stuff to do and had she finished her coffee?

'Just relax, can't you?' she remembered saying.

'I can relax when I'm dead,' he had replied with a laugh.

She could not pretend that his death, in spite of the little warning, had not been one tremendous shock but she would be all right. She wanted to remember Frank as the young man she had married, the young man she had adored, skirting over the latter few years that had been difficult because there was no point in muddying the waters. They loved each other and they would have stuck it out, she knew that, and maybe once he was retired things would have been better. Yes, she was sure they would have been.

She was guilty of keeping secrets from him, of not mentioning the little gifts her mother had given her in the early years to help tide them over. The truth was the business was a modest success but it had fallen short of Frank's grandiose expectations over the years when he had visions of them having an enormous fleet of vans. It needed a little boost now and then and that had come – without anything ever being said – from her private income.

She had a purpose in life now and that was to bring them all through this. Amy was taking it hardest of all but then she always was Daddy's little girl but Mike was proving to be her rock, surprising her in the way he had stepped in to take over the running of the business. He was being helped considerably by Shirley but things were running smoothly and she was grateful to Frank that he had left things in such good order. It was as if he had known his time was limited because the home files kept in his study were in equally good order, with little notes written on them for her. It was those little handwritten notes that got to her and made her cry at first but at the same time they also annoyed her for they could be patronizing, the messages childishly simple so that she might understand them. That was the trouble with Frank; he had never thought her capable of anything that smacked of business. She was reminded now of his comment about the business being up shit creek if Mike had to take over and it suited her fine that he had been totally wrong about that. Without his father watching his every move Mike was a different man and not before time she was proud of him. He had been at her side at the funeral, her support and strength, and she had leaned on him heavily. Amy had been a wreck but there was no man for her to lean on. If she ever set eyes on Brian again she would give him a piece of her mind for treating her daughter so shabbily and at such a dreadful time in her life.

With the business ticking over and a surprisingly full calendar for the next two months they had not yet decided what was going to happen in the future but it was fairly obvious that Mike would not be around for much longer and that the move to France would be going ahead. For the first few months following Frank's death nobody dared mention the French cottage in her hearing but when she asked Monique what was happening she said that everything was fine and that it was being looked after by caretakers until they were ready.

Now that things were settling down a little, Monique, brave girl, had driven down to France to take a preliminary look at the cottage. Knowing Monique she would already be making plans to put her stamp on it. At least this time there would be no Frank to make outrageous comments on her decorating style. Christine had finally dared to look at the only photograph they had of it and had to admit it looked quite delightful.

Slowly and reluctantly, because frankly she had no choice, she was coming to terms with the idea of them moving to France, although acceptance and resignation was not quite the same thing as being happy about it.

Chapter Twelve

The journey had been interesting, driving the length of England and getting down to Dover proving to be the worst bit by far, involving a cheap but cheerless stopover. Monique enjoyed the trip across the channel avoiding the temptation to go into the duty-free shop and as the coast of France appeared and people all around started to point it out she felt, ridiculously, that after all these years she was coming home.

Once off the ferry, the claustrophobic feel of the lower car deck not having been the best experience, the driving in France proved remarkably easy as the roads were so much emptier and as she relaxed, quickly becoming used to driving on the opposite side, something stirred in her memory. One of her earliest recollections was being taken on holiday when she was about four years old to visit Aunt Sylvie in the days when the sisters were on more friendly terms. Maybe she had been driven along these very same roads or was it that the roads in France all looked much the same?

As soon as she realized that she was losing concentration, she booked into a small hotel so that she could rest and make an early start next day. Between them, the receptionist's poor English and her dreadful French they managed to work things out and she was given a lovely single room and later enjoyed a delight of a meal in the little hotel restaurant. The following morning she was up with the lark, opting out of breakfast before setting off a little more confidently and making steady progress.

The Normandy countryside was so lush and at this time of year there were so many apple trees in full bloom. Even the cows were different; brown and white French cows had long-lashed dreamy eyes and an altogether more chic look than their English counterparts. There was no great rush so she consulted her map and guide book and made a detour to visit Claude Monet's house and garden. The flower garden – Clos Normand – at the front of the house took her breath away; full of spring blooms, the perspectives, symmetries and soft warm colours were exactly what she might have expected from such an artistic eye. She loved the freedom Monet gave the flowers and the way he married rare varieties with common plants such as daisies and poppies.

Standing on the walkway of the water garden she watched an American couple busily taking pictures, their voices strident and suddenly offensive to her ears. Monique was not looking so much at the Japanese bridge with its glorious hanging plants but at the reflections underneath it. The morning mist was rising and the gently moving water made the scene come alive and ripple before her eyes. Monet might be long dead but his romantic vision lingered both in his paintings and this garden that he had loved.

It moved her beyond words.

She was French and all this was part of her heritage. She needed to be here, at home; it was where she belonged – in this beautiful country where there was space to spread your wings instead of being pulled in tightly as you were in England. Already the spring warmth was settling on her and seeping into her, so different from the cold Lancashire winds she was used to, for even in high summer that wind from the Fell could still surprise you. There was a bleak beauty in that Fell, however, and she acknowledged that but this altogether softer beauty was what she now craved.

Leaving Giverney behind she got back onto the road and continued her journey. She was in no hurry but she also recognized that there was a certain reluctance to complete the journey, which she could not understand. Perhaps it was something to do with stretching out the anticipation of what she might find when she finally arrived.

Mike had been concerned about her coming here alone but she had no fears. She had studied the route with him and it was fairly straightforward and if all else failed and she became hopelessly lost she could contact her aunt. She had spoken to her on the phone after Christmas, giving her the news of Frank's death and saying that it might be some time before they could come over to take advantage of her wonderful gift.

'Of course, my angel, do not worry. The cottage is there for you whenever you are ready. Madame Perret is looking after it and she is very reliable.' The hesitation was minimal. 'The job at the hotel will still be available for your husband whenever he wishes to take it up. Henri has promised as much and we can rely on him.'

'Are you sure?'

'Absolutely.'

'Won't it matter that Mike can't speak French?'

She knew even if she could not see her that her aunt was giving a shrug.

'He will learn quickly and they have a lot of English visitors so he will help there. Six of one and two of the other, is that it?'

'Not quite.' Monique laughed, reassured that, once he picked up on the language, Mike would be acting as interpreter as well as doing whatever else Henri had in mind for him. Mike was adaptable and now that he was free of his father's controlling ways he was a different man. She liked this new man very much.

'Henri might be hell to live with, a womanizer with a bad temper, but he is an honourable man,' Sylvie continued, though not altogether convincingly, and just for a moment Monique felt a twinge of doubt. They were taking a lot on trust here and she was not entirely sure she could fully count on her aunt.

'Would you thank Henri for us? It would be mad for us to move without the guarantee of a job,' Monique told her, peeved nonetheless that by dying at the wrong moment her father-in-law was, in death, putting obstacles in the way of what ought to have been a smooth process. They should have been installed in the cottage by now as they could have left their house in Christine's capable hands. The house in River Terrace was up for sale but it would prove awkward if it sold any time soon. If that happened they would have to use delaying tactics. She did not care to be camping out at the cottage whilst they did it up although she did not think Mike would mind. No, she would only move in when it was ready, beautifully decorated and filled with a mix of the very best French and English furniture she could find. Judging from the photograph, there was nothing she wanted to change about the outside, which was charming. Sylvie had said it was sound so it would mainly be cosmetic work on the interior and the prospect of a blank canvas on which she could really go to town and beyond was a joy.

Christine had said they could move in with her if necessary but that was the last thing she wanted because she needed to start backing away from her mother-in-law and if Sol got wind of that plan he was capable of causing real problems.

Of course she was sorry Frank had died. The family had been predictably devastated and she saw her role very much as supporting Mike, who in turn took on the role of senior member of the household with some verve. He was younger than Amy but oddly Amy did not seem to mind that it was Mike who took charge, arranging the funeral, doing the lot, in fact, whilst she just sat around looking numb.

The funeral had been held at a church on the outskirts of

Preston, never mind that Frank had been a stranger to it, followed by burial in the churchyard there. It was a family plot and they stood around on a bitingly chill day early in the New Year, with a good turnout of some far-flung members of the Fletcher clan, some of whom she recalled from her wedding.

Amy, with that disastrous short hair, wore a black suit with a long, dark grey coat covering it. She looked awful, her eyes red-rimmed from crying, more of a hindrance than a help to her mother, who was remarkably composed throughout. Although it was a difficult time of year, that dead period between Christmas and New Year when everybody forgot what day it was, Monique found a fantastic coat for the funeral at her favourite vintage shop; an understated black coat lifted by an enormous fluffy fur collar. Teaming it with black leather boots and a tiny black pillbox hat, she felt very Jackie Kennedy. Under the coat she wore a simple black shift dress and under that, black underwear. Well, honestly, if you were going to do a thing, do it with some style. Amy's dark grey and Christine's navy simply did not cut the mustard. She alone looked the part of chief mourner.

'I love your coat, Monica,' one of Christine's friends exclaimed, only to be instantly shushed because the casual remark was inappropriate to the sombreness of the scene. 'The collar is so pretty, so soft. You could swear it was real fur.'

It *was* real fur but admitting such a politically incorrect thing was out of the question, not at Frank's funeral, not as his coffin was about to be lowered reverently into the grave and she was not going to correct the woman's mistake about her name either. She thought she had conducted herself well, dutifully allowing a few tears to spill over during the service. She sat in the front pew beside Amy, who sobbed noisily throughout, great uncontrolled hiccups, and really rather let herself down. Monique had not liked Frank so it was insulting to suddenly change her tune and become heartbroken even if it meant that the move to the cottage in France had to be deferred until things were a little calmer. Mike was refusing to leave his mother just now and she rather liked the way he had put his foot down for once.

The months following the disastrous Christmas passed in a whirl, providing her with a further problem that she could not bear to think about. She briefly met up with Sol in January. His concern for her had been both surprising and touching – maybe he did have feelings for her after all – although he had got the wrong end of the stick in imagining that she was heartbroken by Frank's death. The consoling he had offered had been rather nice, though, and had of course delayed her decision to break it off completely before it became a hopeless entanglement that she could not escape from. The truth was she was dithering about breaking it off because deep down, she did not really want to.

She had not seen him since then but he was refusing to take no for an answer and was becoming careless in his attempts to contact her; it was just a matter of time before it was out in the open. You could only keep a secret for so long so she needed to get out of his hair completely and she could only do that by moving as far away as possible.

She drove slowly and carefully, pulling off the road from time to time just to stretch her legs and sniff the wonderful French air, for even that felt different. She imagined she would have much more room to play with at the cottage than her present home and although she wanted to take some of her belongings with her, she was keen to create a new look for it. Frank Fletcher's teasing remark on first seeing her living room at River Terrace had hit her hard and she was not going to make that mistake again. Amy was threatening to visit in summer – if they were settled in by then – and she wanted to have things organized, everything perfect because for some reason she wanted Amy to like it. She was aware that Amy was making an effort with Mike and she knew that her sister-in-law appreciated the way Mike had helped her through that initial grief that had engulfed her far more than it had them. Amy, much to her surprise, had been the one to let it all out whereas Christine had remained stoic and a little aloof and never once let her guard down.

It was a shame for Amy that the thing with Brian had not lasted but looking back she was not surprised and she recalled that the last she saw of him he was accompanying Amy down to the hospital café. She was sitting with Christine in the corridor outside the ward because the screen round Frank's bed had been pulled across and the nurses were attending him. When Amy returned, alone, they were still sitting in the corridor, a little concerned at the amount of time it was taking to do whatever it was they were doing behind that screen.

'Where's Brian?' Christine asked and Monique knew at once from Amy's casual shrug what had happened. He had chickened out of this awful situation and abandoned her. Brian was a little like Sol – too handsome for his own good – and she supposed she was guilty of flirting a little with him on that Christmas Eve but then that was what she did and it never really meant anything.

Standing by the window on that Christmas Day afternoon, watching the others depart, she did not regret her decision to stay indoors, giving a shudder before going to sit on the opposite sofa to Brian. She tucked her legs up under her, the folds of her dress demurely hiding any glimpse of leg. She had always played cover-up, knowing that excited a man far more than large displays of flesh.

'Is it serious between you two?' she asked, giving him a cheeky smile.

'No. It's just a casual thing.' He smiled too, legs wide

apart in that way of the alpha-male, relaxed and suddenly a little dangerous. He was just like Sol, the sort who thought he was a magnet for women and although she could be tempted she had no intention of allowing him even a small victory. She had shut down and regretted the previous evening's flirtatious behaviour. She must stop doing that.

'Amy's very keen on her career.' She reached for a mint chocolate, nibbled at it. 'Don't let it go on too long,' she urged him, suddenly and inexplicably feeling that she had to protect her sister-in-law from this man. She had seen the looks they had exchanged and it seemed as if Amy liked him a lot. 'I don't want to see her hurt,' she added, irritated that he should laugh at that.

'Since when do you care what happens to her? You make it pretty clear that you don't get on with any of them, except your husband, obviously.'

'It's difficult to fit into a family when you first come into it,' she said. 'You're an outsider and they always resent you a little and as a matter of fact you're wrong. I might not get on with Frank or Amy but I do get on very well with Christine. I haven't any family of my own,' she went on. 'So they are all I have.' It was a surprising admission as much to herself as to him and it made her feel rather emotional. It was true, for she could not count on her father any more and she rarely saw her aunt. 'You wouldn't know what I'm talking about as you don't have family. Or do you?' She glanced at him and was just in time to catch his guilty look before he tried to disguise it with another smile. 'God, you do have family, don't you? Don't tell me you're married? Divorced?'

There was a short silence and out in the hall the clock chimed the hour.

'As near as divorced,' he said at last. 'Can I trust you, Monique, not to say anything until I've had the chance to tell her?'

She let him sweat a moment before nodding.

'I won't tell her. But don't leave it too long unless you intend her to be your second wife.'

'No fear. Once bitten and all that.... She's not expecting that either.'

He got up and put another log on the fire. It sizzled, an orange flame bursting forth.

Well, well. She was privy to a secret and she would avoid Amy when she returned just in case she accidentally let something slip. She had promised not to say anything but honestly, he had a cheek asking that of her. It was in Amy's best interests that she should know and, promise notwithstanding, she had a duty to tell her.

In the event she had no time to do anything about it because, out on the hill, unknown to them Frank was at that very moment succumbing to his final illness.

She stayed overnight in another hotel, unable to practise her newly buffed up French as the proprietor spoke perfect English. He knew the village where she was going and when she asked if it was pretty he smiled and nodded, though not altogether convincingly.

When she arrived she saw why.

The approach through an avenue of the ubiquitous poplars was impressive but once they fizzled out it became little more than a dirt track as she passed cottages and bigger properties in varying states of disrepair as if there had been a sudden exodus years ago and people had not returned. It was also eerily quiet. She carefully manoeuvred the car round potholes, narrowly missing the bigger stones and having to stop at one point when a cow appeared, alone and worried-looking, firmly lodged in the middle of the track. It was a large creature and it stood its ground a minute, as did she, until it turned its back on her, offering a wonderful view of its magnificent rear before sloping off.

Dark clouds had started to build and it began to rain, big plops at first on the windscreen of her little car. She acknowledged that she would not be seeing the village at its best but as she passed the name-sign at last – muddied and leaning at an angle – she saw that it was nothing like some of the other villages she had driven through. The sun was shining earlier and those villages had been bustling places with the women wearing summery dresses already, bare-legged, carrying baskets, smiling and chatting, each of them accompanied by small children. She stopped at one of those villages, buying bread, cheese, butter, eggs, milk and coffee, proud to be practising her French on the lady in the shop. She very nearly confessed to being French – *je suis française* she could say and it was quite true but her vocabulary was still lacking and she did not have the nerve to start what might become a difficult conversation.

There was nobody about in the village she was now in, although the onset of rain could explain that but the houses themselves were a disappointment and the whole village was surrounded by flat fields and nothing much of interest. She had the scrap of paper with the caretaker's address and parking up outside the house she walked up the path and knocked on the door. There was no immediate reply and although she was reluctant to knock a second time she did so. She knew there was somebody inside for she sensed a movement and shuffles behind the door.

Stupidly, she had no umbrella with her so by the time the door was opened – after much pulling back of stiff locks and chains – she was drenched. The woman who opened the door looked at her with mild interest as, haltingly, Monique explained that she was the niece of Madame Sylvie Roye and had come to collect the key for the cottage. Her aunt had telephoned ahead to tell them that she was expected, had she not?

'Oui, madame.' The woman whose name she could not for the moment remember did not smile nor did she invite her in. The rain had stepped up a gear and was now verging on torrential and Monique's long silky skirt was clinging

to her legs. The woman, clad entirely in black and looking as if she would be a dead cert for the role of surly French peasant indicated she would be back in a moment. Monique, standing in the rain and not wanting to step uninvited over the threshold could hear cries of exasperation from the woman and an unseen man, hear sounds of drawers being opened and closed before the woman returned holding a large important-looking key. Silently, she reached for a coat and a little belatedly a large black umbrella, which she handed to Monique.

'Il n'est pas loins; suivez moi.'

'Merci, madame.'

So it wasn't far, thank God. Holding the umbrella aloft, Monique followed her a short distance along a path. It was too narrow for them to walk side by side and the woman walked surprisingly fast, skirting puddles in her clumpy boots and muttering as she did so. Monique, flustered by the language problem and working out in her head what she might be called upon to say next was relieved when the path widened out and she saw a cottage of the prettier variety very like the one in the photograph set a little back behind a fence and tiny garden. As they drew closer, she saw that it was indeed the cottage in the photograph.

But no. The woman walked on, turning up another lane. She could hear voices and a dog barking and then the woman stopped so abruptly that she very nearly careered into her, stabbing her in the head unfortunately with the umbrella.

'Sorry,' she said at once, mortified as the woman turned to glare at her, rubbing her scalp before flinging out her arm and pointing.

Monique followed her gaze. For a moment she could not think what to say and when she did think of something she spoke in English so that the woman looked blank.

She gathered herself together and smiled.

'Madame Perret … ' the name came to her suddenly as

they stood close together sheltering under the umbrella as the rain showed no sign of relenting. She was wearing flat pumps and her bare feet were uncomfortably damp now. The pitter-patter of the rain was loud on the umbrella fabric and she wondered if the woman was deaf, for she was now holding her head to one side pointing her left ear towards Monique. *'Il doit y avoir une erreur,'* Monique said slowly hoping for the best as she waited for a sign of recognition in the woman's eyes.

'Non, il n'y a pas d'erreur – comme ça,' she said, handing over the key.

'Really?' Monique stared again at the house. There was no mistake, then, this was it but it was nothing like the idyllic-looking cottage in the photograph.

This cottage was a complete wreck.

The key sat heavily in her handbag as Monique drove on, the rain easing and the sun coming out as she left the village behind. That figured somehow. It was a chill place, the sort of place that you would drive through quickly if you came across it by accident. It would be the perfect setting for one of those disturbing French films shot in black and white, the cast an unwholesome mix of sexy and sinister. There was a row of shops including a patisserie, a pharmacy and a small café and as she drove out she saw there was also an inn but the shutters were drawn and it did not look the least bit welcoming, so she booked into a hotel about ten miles away because she could not possibly stay in the damp dirty hovel that was the cottage. She tried to ring her aunt but she was not answering.

She could not get Mike on his phone either, her own mobile suddenly taking leave of its senses in this Godforsaken place, and she did not feel up to using the hotel phone with her limited French. She needed to collect her thoughts anyway before she rang Mike for she would come over as frantic and incoherent and that was the last thing she wanted.

At least she had a soft bed and clean sheets here in this inn and she would have a meal later in the little dining room she had glimpsed as she was shown up to her room by a friendly lady, who had expressed concern at her bedraggled state. She was so wet that she left a little puddle on the wooden hall floor for which she apologized although the woman had waved that aside with a smile.

She hastily stripped off her damp clothes and took a wonderfully hot shower before changing, wringing out her wet things and leaving them to dry. Lying down at last, fully clothed on top of the bed she felt tears pricking her eyelids, real tears this time.

This was not how it was supposed to be; this was a nightmare. She wanted Mike beside her with his reassuringly solid presence and his pragmatic take on life. Her stupidly romantic dream was rapidly diminishing as she faced up to reality. It was not going to happen; her dream of living out her life in idyllic style somewhere where the sun always shone and where they could eat wonderful fresh food and drink glorious French wine was rapidly diminishing.

She was being utterly pathetic, she thought, as she searched through her bag for a tissue to blow her nose. She pushed at her hair, damp from the shower, and sat on the edge of the bed trying to get her thoughts in order.

Think, Monique, think.

But she could not, not just now. She was tired and feeling a bit sick but then, she was pregnant and what could you expect?

Chapter Thirteen

There was a round of applause led by Mr Armitage as Amy and Daniel entered the room. Mr Theodore – Teddy – Armitage was a short, bald-headed gentleman with black-framed spectacles, as nattily dressed as ever wearing a pin-stripe suit and waistcoat, a white shirt and a blue bow tie. He beamed and patted Daniel on the back as they came forward before shaking Amy's hand profusely. She liked Mr Armitage, you could not help but like him, but there was no denying his lack of business acumen and she hoped the changes Daniel had put in place would shake him up, although she had severe doubts they would. He was a gentleman of the old school much respected in the organization and in a way it would be a sad day when he retired, signalling the end of a more relaxed era. He had led the company through difficult times in the past and she suspected he was just choosing the right moment to bow out gracefully before he was stabbed to retail death by the pleasant-faced men and women around him.

The buffet table was heaving with a selection of goodies courtesy of the restaurant staff and there were more than enough bottles of wine. Amy decided she would stick to bottled water as she would need a clear head for this evening and whatever that might bring. Janet had booked a table for two at Gardner's, the fancy restaurant Daniel had mentioned, looking inquiringly at Amy as she informed her about it.

'It's business,' Amy had told her quickly. 'Nothing more than that.'

'Of course it is. But he is a lovely man and unattached, that's all I'm saying.'

'What about Bea?'

'What *about* Bea?' Janet smiled. 'She's not his type, Amy. I've seen Mr Coleridge looking at you sometimes and I could swear that he's not thinking of you as a colleague.'

'Janet, don't even start on that,' she said. 'I've told you, it's just business.'

In that case why was she hoping to avoid Bea this afternoon and why, if they did chat, had she decided not to mention that she was being taken out to Gardner's this evening? It was a bit of a worry, frankly, for there was no need to go out to an expensive restaurant to talk business. If he had something to say he could have said it this morning when she was helping him clear out the office. Not least it was causing her a headache because she could not decide what would be suitable to wear. Nothing too sexy, obviously, as she did not wish to put her bosom on display in the only truly smart cocktail dress she possessed but she could hardly turn up for a meal there in one of her work suits and the all-occasion dress she had was black and she was fed up to the back teeth with that. She had a full afternoon ahead of her and there would be no time to buy anything new so she would have to dig something up.

The speeches began well, for Mr Armitage was nothing if not an accomplished orator. Following his little offering, short but very much to the point, it seemed that each departmental head had been called upon to chip in with their pennyworth. Mercifully, none of them hugged the limelight although when it came to Bea's turn she did sashay up to the front, pausing a moment to take in the room and looking as if she was about to accept an Oscar. She was wearing a navy suit today, a broad, silver-buckled belt emphasizing her slim waist, and her blonde hair was swept up, her only jewellery small pearl earrings.

'Thank you, Marcus ... I would just like to add my personal thanks to Daniel,' she gushed in that low, husky, undeniably sexy voice of hers. Amy was amused to see the men roundabout rearranging their demeanour into that tough-as-you-like male stance in an all-out effort to be the one to impress when confronted by a beautiful woman. Glancing at Daniel, however, she did not see this in him; rather a relaxed smile as he acknowledged a little ruefully the tribute coming his way. 'I think we all deserve a pat on the back,' Bea continued, her glance sweeping the room. 'I know we have all worked incredibly hard these past few months and Langdales has never looked as good as it did at Christmas. In Cosmetics & Perfumery we had an incredibly successful autumn/winter season and we are planning huge promotions over the coming spring/summer season that will keep us on track.' She smiled broadly, cheeks flushed before consulting the sheet of paper she had with her.

Amy hid a smile. In a minute she would be thanking her parents, her stylist, her hairdresser and God knows who else.

'I remember coming to this store when I was a little girl,' Bea continued just as they were all thinking the pause had gone on too long. 'And I loved it then, particularly coming through the doors into what, back then, I thought was the smelly bit.'

They obligingly laughed but she was not done yet.

'We pride ourselves on being a family here at Langdales,' Bea went on earnestly, oblivious to the fidgeting now amongst the staff. 'And when a family member leaves we all feel the pain so, Daniel ... ' the further dramatic pause was worthy of Meryl Streep herself. 'We shall miss you very much but we wish you well in your new career and we will do our utmost not to let you down.'

Mr Armitage jumped in then, urging another round of applause before inviting them to enjoy the buffet.

'I don't think she had quite finished,' Daniel murmured, for Amy's ears alone.

Amy merely smiled, moving away and heading purposefully towards the others before she could be accosted by Bea.

'Does that boss of yours ever wear a suit?' Marcus of Menswear collared her. 'You would think today of all days he would make a bloody effort.'

'Shush.' Amy collected a few titbits on her plate and allowed him to steer her away.

'What's going to happen to you now?' Marcus was good looking in a sharp, dark-haired Italian way. He was shorter than her when she was wearing heels. 'Will you be staying?'

'I'm not sure,' she said. 'It depends.'

'I'm surprised he isn't taking you with him. You make a good team.'

'I'm sure he's more than capable of going it alone,' she said, watching him with Bea who was laughing and standing very close to him. Did they look as if they were lovers? Was it possible to tell? Certainly Daniel had never given any indication but then she had learned early on that he was not one for discussing private matters so perhaps he was being remarkably discreet. Whereas keeping things close to his chest had irritated beyond belief where her relationship with Brian had been concerned she had never let it concern her that Daniel was a private person.

But then it was completely different because Daniel was her boss and it was the naffest thing imaginable to get yourself into a hot situation with your boss.

'Let me know how you get on and good luck, Amy, with whatever you do.' Marcus smiled at her and she reflected on what a nice guy he was. It was no secret that he was gay and in a long-term relationship and she was glad for him. As Marcus was led away she found herself alone a minute amongst the people milling around the buffet. She had no appetite and discreetly got rid of her plate on the buffet table. There was going to be an awful lot of food left over, she thought, ridiculously concerned at the wastage, but then at these functions you never liked to look as if you were stuffing yourself.

Much as she tried to avoid it, a one-to-one with Bea was inevitable before the little goodbye party ended and they all headed off, back to their respective departments.

'That went very well, didn't it?' Bea said, surprisingly hesitant and seeming to look for reassurance. She was carrying a large glass of white wine and even at close quarters her make-up was pitch-perfect, making Amy conscious of her own shortcomings in that department.

'It went very well,' Amy said. 'You made a moving speech.'

'Thank you. That means a lot to me.' Bea's bleached white teeth shone a moment. 'I worked on it for ages. I hate speaking in front of people.'

'Do you?' Amy felt a sudden surge of sympathy. 'Well, in that case, you were great, Bea,' she assured her. 'I would never have known.'

'You're very good at presentations. I'm surprised Mr Armitage didn't ask you to say a few words,' Bea said, pinning her in a corner as people started to leave. 'What's happening with you now that Daniel's leaving? Are you staying?'

'Marcus has just asked me that,' she replied. 'And the truth is I'm not sure. Between you and me … ' she lowered her voice, amazed to find herself confessing anything to Bea. 'Keep it to yourself but I've applied for a job over in Preston.'

'Oh, that's where you come from, isn't it?'

She nodded. 'Quite near there. You know that I lost my father at Christmas?'

'I do know.' Bea's face buckled. 'Heaps of sympathy and all that. It must have been horrendous.'

'It was. Still is.' She bit her lip. 'I need to help my mother a bit more and that's the reason I applied for it so that I'll be closer to home. I don't think the store there is a patch on this to be honest but—' She stopped as it occurred that her heart was not really in it and that probably meant that, second interview notwithstanding, they had seen through her and she had not got it.

'Daniel's moving to the northwest,' Bea told her with a sigh. 'I was hoping that maybe he would ask me to go with him.' She looked different suddenly, reminding Amy of the dream because when all the outer gloss was stripped away Bea was essentially a vulnerable woman in love with a man who maybe was not in love with her.

'Has he said anything?' she probed gently. 'Are you and he together?'

So much for discretion. She wished she could take back the question but it was already asked and it was too late.

Bea raised her perfectly plucked eyebrows. 'Not so you would notice. He's been hurt, you know, and men like him are very reluctant to commit to another relationship. I'm giving him space but I'm running out of time if he does shoot off to Manchester.'

'Manchester?'

'Hasn't he told you?'

'No, not exactly.' She knew he was setting up his own business but had assumed it would be based here or hereabouts.

Bea raised her eyebrows. 'I thought he would have told *you*.'

'Why should he? Incidentally ... ' she was just about to tell her about the dinner date, feeling suddenly obligated to do so but Bea cut her off and with that familiar half-wave of hers headed away.

By Bea's own startling admission, she and Daniel were not an item.

And why on earth should that make any difference?

And why on earth did she find herself walking back to the office with a new-found spring in her step?

Chapter Fourteen

The way Frank had talked the business up at commercial events you would be forgiven for thinking that they had a staff of more than a thousand when the reality was that, although they were well up the ladder from the 'man-with-van' set-up, they were not yet in the class of the big-timers in the removal business. The problem was that they had to be damned sure they had a full book before they started on any expansion plans and so they operated on a tight turn-around schedule, content with the number of vans, large and small, that were parked in their yard.

Their full-time staff had mostly been with them for years but just when they needed to consolidate and take stock now that Frank was gone they were about to lose one of the full-time employees. Christine was annoyed because you would think that Shirley would have the sensitivity not to leave them in the lurch at such a difficult time. She was one of those people who had over the years developed her own way of dealing with things, which for her worked very well but the system left the rest of them completely bewildered. Christine had intended to have a serious talk to her about all this so, following Shirley's letter of resignation, she was at least saved that bother.

'I was going to hand in my notice straight after Christmas, Mrs Fletcher,' Shirley said, visibly pale after giving the news. 'And because of what happened I've hung on a bit but

I can't wait any longer, I'm afraid. Jerry needs me to help out at the caravan site; I'm moving into the house there and it's just not on to be commuting every day.'

It was not that far and easily commutable but Christine took the point that she was trying her best to make excuses and if that was the case then there was nothing more to be said.

'You will be missed,' she said, seeing the sadness in the other woman's eyes. She realized that she had really cared for Frank, although she was going to draw a line under that and would not dream of asking her any personal questions. Jerry was her long-suffering partner and she was making the best of things.

'You'll manage, Mrs Fletcher. You've worked here and you know the ropes. It's not rocket science. It's all fairly straightforward – answering the phone, booking appointments and keeping a check on the diary and chasing up accounts, of course. Then there's the storage facility. That has to be checked regularly and the vans have to—'

'Yes I do know how everything works,' Christine interrupted with a small smile. 'I'll sit down with you tomorrow and we can go through your system,' she added pointedly. 'Mike has some new ideas he wants to try out but as you know he'll be leaving us soon so I suppose I'll take over until we can get a new manager appointed.'

'It will give you something to think about,' Shirley said. 'They say that when you lose somebody suddenly like you lost Mr Fletcher, it helps to keep busy. What you don't want to be doing is sitting around twiddling your thumbs. He thought the world of you, did Mr Fletcher and he often told me that.'

'Did he?' She was surprised and suspicious at the same time. She looked round the office and suddenly realized that it was looking the worse for wear. They did most of the bookings over the phone but people did sometimes pop in to check their nearby storage area, which meant they came into this office and the first impression mattered. Shirley had papers scattered all over the place, a lot of stuff was sitting on the floor and there was a battered tray full of mugs beside a kettle that had seen better days. All in all it looked grubby and that was enough to put people off. How had she not noticed how awful it looked?

Mike thought they ought to send flyers out to student accommodation offering an additional cheap 'man-with-van' type service because students only had bits of furniture and stuff. They had always steered away from minor moves like that in the past but if it kept a couple of the smaller vans in business then why not? Mike also thought they should be targeting commercial moves more because that, too, was something they had always shied away from. He wanted to appoint a project manager to deal specifically with this area, for relocating a commercial business was quite different from a domestic move. They needed somebody to organize the dismantling and reassembling of office furniture and to do it at the weekend to minimize disruption and to offer guarantees in the transfer of sensitive office equipment. Stealth and efficiency was the name of the game there, which was why Frank had considered it to be more trouble than it was worth.

Mike thought they ought to update the tired website, make it more attractive and accessible and Mike thought....

Mike thought.

Mike should have been putting these ideas of his forward to his father when he was still alive, for that's what he had been willing him to do and it saddened her that their son was so cowed by his father that he could not voice these thoughts of his, some of which had serious commercial viability.

Christine still could not get hold of Monique and hoped she was all right. She stopped by the house on River Terrace on her way home from the office, letting herself in with a key and dumping the shopping in the kitchen. Mike was not brilliant at cooking and she had offered to prepare his meals for him whilst Monique was away.

She would do anything to avoid going back to Snape House and the empty rooms. It was strange because she had been alone there most of the time even when Frank was alive but now for the first time the sheer size of the place was overwhelming to her. She really was rattling around like a pea in a drum and before long when Mike was gone to France it would be even worse.

It was early days, everybody kept reminding her of that, and the ladies of the village and the church ladies had been particularly kind in turning up with food offerings as if by losing Frank she had lost the ability to cook. Flowers, too, which she much appreciated and, glad of their company, she would drag them in off the doorstep and make coffee and sit them down for a chat hoping they would not set her off with their tear-filled eyes.

She was, she was told, bearing up well.

In the kitchen at River Terrace, she got to work preparing a chicken casserole and an apple pie for herself and her son. Working in another woman's kitchen was not easy, not only because you had no idea where anything was but also because she was not used to a gas oven and was a bit uncertain of cooking times.

Monique had some lovely rustic pots, she thought, bending down and searching through the cupboards and as she straightened she looked at the big framed poster on the wall. Monique had had that poster for a long time so it was pure coincidence but Christine imagined that the kitchen at Monique's French cottage would look just like the one in the poster with the back door open and the sunlight pouring through. A solid table sat in the middle of the poster kitchen; on it was a selection of French produce, shiny green apples and cheese and a baguette. It looked as if the owner had suddenly popped out, for there was a tantalizing glimpse through the open door of a flower-filled garden. It was all a little different in reality as she swivelled round from looking at the poster to gaze out of the kitchen window. There were few flowers in Mike and Monique's tiny rear garden as they had paved it with grey and pink slabs, putting a table and chairs out there although you could count the days last summer when the weather had been good enough to eat outside on one hand.

Putting the last of the ingredients in the casserole, Christine washed her hands and dried them, wondering where Monique was and what she was doing. Perhaps Mike had had some luck reaching her but a worry caught at her that maybe something was wrong. Monique was an attractive young woman, travelling alone and there were some very strange people about. She should have gone with her but the offer was never made and she hadn't liked to push it forward.

Mike was going to try ringing the French aunt this evening if he still could not get hold of his wife; he did not seem unduly concerned but then when it came to worrying, Christine knew she was in a class of her own. She had worried herself sick after Frank's first illness and by God, she had been right to do so.

The phone in the hall rang as she was peeling apples for the pie – English Bramley apples, of course – and she hastily wiped her hands on her apron and hurried to answer it.

'Hello, darling … ' a man said before she could say a word and then after the briefest pause. 'Hello …?'

'Who is this?' she asked, tempted to hang up but giving him the benefit of the doubt, for he might have made a genuine mistake. 'Do you have the right number?'

'Obviously not.' There was the smallest of laughs. 'I do apologize.'

'That's all right,' she said, warming a little because he did have a lovely voice.

However, the call unsettled her. For instance, he had

not seemed particularly surprised and had not asked what the number was, nor had he said what number he meant to ring as she usually did if she inadvertently misdialled. Curious, she tapped in 1471 and a number came through, a local number, an easy to remember number. How could she find out who that was and why on earth would she want to anyway? It was simply a wrong number and she must not read any more into it.

Thank God Mike had a message when he got back. It was a brief message via Aunt Sylvie to say that Monique had managed to contact her and was all right and was staying a while at a hotel in the village adjacent to the cottage. There was, as he had suspected, a problem with her mobile reception.

'I've got the number of the hotel,' he said, coming into the kitchen and sniffing appreciatively. 'But I haven't rung yet because I have to work out what I'm going to say in case they don't speak English.'

'They all speak English,' she said confidently.

'They do in the big hotels in Paris,' he said, 'but this is a one-horse town by the sound of it and they might not. In any case it's a bit of a cheek to make that assumption, surely? How's your French, Mum? Do you feel up to ringing and asking to speak to her? We can do it between us.'

'All right, we can give it a try,' Christine said, turning to smile at him. 'How did you get on this afternoon? Do they want us to do the move?'

'Yes and they were delighted with the figure I quoted although it was a rock-bottom price. I think we'll get Ian to take charge of it. They have a reasonable amount of stuff and they want us to pack everything for them. The problem is access at the other end so if we use one of the big vans we'll have to trundle things up a narrow track, which is going to take time, but I've allowed for that. They seem reasonably happy with the deal.'

She nodded; talking shop was oh so familiar and oddly comforting. Very few of their removals were completely hassle free – there was always some problem or other to deal with, often an unforeseen snag – but it was part and parcel of the business and very little fazed them. She reckoned their drivers were the best in the business. Some of their cockier drivers seemed to delight in achieving a scratch-free delivery up the narrowest of lanes and round the tightest of corners.

'Any more interest in *your* house?' she asked, conscious of the For Sale board that was nailed to the front wall. Ridiculously she hoped there was not. Her hope, deeply hidden, for it was entirely selfish, was that there would be no interest whatsoever, that the idea of moving to France would suddenly lose its momentum and, if they had a chance to take stock, they might realize that life here was not so bad after all.

'Oh yes, I forgot to tell you. The agents did a viewing yesterday and apparently this couple are dead keen. They have nothing to sell so there's no chain and it could go ahead pretty quickly.'

'Great,' she said, trying to drum up enthusiasm to match his, switching back to shop-talk because that topic was too painful. 'We'll need to get the interviews arranged for the new manager before Shirley goes because I'd like her to sit in on them – and you, of course.'

'Three of us?' He smiled wryly. 'That's a bit intense, isn't it? I thought we'd agreed that Howard's the man to step in. I have every confidence in him, Mum, and Dad liked him.' His face puckered a little, not so anyone but a mother would notice.

'You're probably right but I think we must go through the motions,' she said, checking on the casserole. She would go home later to the empty house and probably have a little private weep because, even though lately Frank had irritated the hell out of her, it was just awful without him.

After their meal they tried without success to get hold of Monique. Maybe Mike had been given the wrong number as the hotel phone was dead and there was no answer either from Aunt Sylvie's number. Christine could tell that her own anxiety was beginning to transmit to Mike.

'Should we call the police?' she asked.

'Good heavens, Mum, there's no need for that. That's called panicking. She said she was all right in her message to Sylvie.'

'I think you should go over,' she told him. 'You can set off tomorrow and be there in no time.'

'And there speaks someone who thinks we're moving to the ends of the earth,' he said, teasing her gently whilst considering the suggestion. 'I might do that if I can get it organized. I've got the name of the hotel at least so I can find her. These bloody phones,' he said, staring glumly at his mobile. 'We've got so dependent on them that we've forgotten how hard it used to be to keep in touch with somebody when they were out of the country. I'm sure she's fine, Mum,' he added. 'She can take care of herself. She's stronger than she looks.'

Christine was unconvinced. Monique was naive, a rare quality these days, and she worried for her.

She left soon afterwards and drove back to Snape House. Daylight was just beginning to fade and the first thing she did was to switch on the radio and turn on as many lights as possible. She had moved into another bedroom, feeling that she could not sleep in the bed she and Frank had shared for so many years and so had made up the bed in the room Amy used, finding the blue colour scheme soothing. Amy had taken to ringing every night at precisely eight o'clock but tonight it was a little earlier.

'Have you eaten?' was the first thing she asked, making Christine smile because her children as well as the ladies of the village seemed to imagine that she was starving herself.

'I've eaten with Mike. Chicken casserole and rice,' she said. 'And apple pie and cream to follow.'

'Well done. You've got to keep your strength up.'

Christine held back a sharp retort because she meant well and was obviously concerned about her.

'I'm going out for dinner later,' Amy went on. 'But I'm all ready so I can talk a while. Are you sure you're okay, Mum?'

'Absolutely fine.' She smiled firmly into the phone. 'I wish you two would stop fussing. I'm fine but we're a bit worried about Monique because temporarily we seem to have lost contact.'

'She's still in France then?'

'That's right. Her mobile's off and we can't get through to the hotel but Mike's had a message from her aunt in Paris to say that Monique has been in touch with her.'

'Well then, what's the problem? Monique is stronger than she looks.'

'Funny. That's exactly what Mike said. Anyway I think he's going to go to France tomorrow and see what's what. He needs to see the cottage himself and we can keep things moving at work without him.'

'I'm sure you can.'

Christine detected a faint sniff and was anxious to put her right. 'He's been doing very well, love, since your dad died. Everything is going swimmingly and not only that, he's come up with a load of new ideas. I hate to say it but we've been stuck in a rut for a while and it's good to see him so upbeat.'

'Really? That's marvellous.'

She could sense Amy was getting ready to hang up so Christine stepped in quickly.

'Who are you going out with tonight?'

'My old boss Daniel. You remember me telling you about him?'

'I think so.'

'It's not a proper date,' Amy said with a little laugh. 'He wants to talk business but he's taking me to a very nice restaurant to do it.'

'Sounds like a date to me.' Christine sighed. 'Be careful, darling. You've had one disappointment already with Brian. I know you were starting to make plans.'

'No I was not. I don't know where you get these ideas from. I've not lost any sleep over him, Mum. I might have known he wouldn't last the distance and when I found out he had kids and hadn't told me that was the last straw. Can you believe that?'

'I can believe anything of a man, darling. The least he could have done was stay a while to support you over Christmas. It was despicable of him to leave you like that. Talk about bad timing.'

'Forget him.' Amy sounded annoyed. 'Is anybody there with you?'

'No of course not. Why?'

'Just wondered. Are you *very* lonely, Mum?'

'What a question! No I don't think so. It takes a bit of getting used to, that's all.'

'It would be better if you had neighbours.'

'I do have neighbours down in the village.'

'Yes but they're not that close. What if something happened in the middle of the night?'

'Stop it. I am not in my dotage yet. Look, darling, this is getting a little wearing. Would you please stop worrying about me?'

'I'm thinking of coming over at the weekend if that's all right?'

'Lovely. We can go shopping or is that too much like work for you?'

'Of course we can go shopping,' Amy echoed. 'I need some new spring stuff so you can help me choose it and while we're at it we'll get you some new clothes as well. We both need cheering up. Look, Mum, I'm sorry but I have to go. Daniel's picking me up in ten minutes and I still haven't decided which coat I'm wearing.'

'Ring me tomorrow and enjoy yourself, darling, on your *business* date.' She laughed as she replaced the receiver. Business date at a fancy restaurant? Who was kidding whom?

She had picked up the free paper from the mat when she arrived home. Usually she just tossed it in the bin but it was sitting on the kitchen table as she made herself a pot of tea following Amy's call so she sat a moment and idly leafed through it.

There was a miscellaneous sales page and she found herself going through it smiling at some of the entries. Oh look, somebody was selling a world globe for forty pounds, one of the sort Frank had always wanted and had never got round to buying. She had once considered getting him one for a birthday but again, when it came to it, she had settled for something useful like a shirt or a jumper. Thinking of that reminded her of him, as so many little things did, and she took a deep, steadying breath because she did not want to start on a crying session which was only wearying and ultimately useless.

There was nothing else of interest in the paper, just a few notices of coming events and a page of adverts for local shops but it was then, as she glanced at that page, that she recognized the telephone number. It was one of those easy to remember numbers ending in triple three and she noted that it belonged to a second-hand bookshop over in Lancaster. Why would a man from a second-hand bookshop be ringing Monique and calling her darling? But then it had been a wrong number so he had not actually been ringing her.

Instinctively she knew he had. This man could be an old friend because Monique had been brought up in Lancaster and this old friend could be one of those kind of people who call all and sundry darling without it meaning a thing but she did not recall Monique ever talking about a friend with a bookshop, which was odd because Christine enjoyed nothing more than rifling through the shelves of such establishments. Monique had seen her do it often enough in Preston so why hadn't she mentioned it?

She stopped thinking such thoughts and laughed at herself. Her mind was on overdrive and she was being perfectly ridiculous. Monique was happily married and she was not the sort of girl who would take on a lover. Although Frank had brought that daft idea up once or twice, hadn't she been the one to strenuously deny it?

Nevertheless, daft or not, the next time she was in Lancaster she might just check out that bookshop and see the man who owned that rather pleasant voice.

Chapter Fifteen

Gardner's was in a nondescript side street but then its reputation was such that it did not need to advertise its presence.

Before ringing her mother for the brief phone chat, Amy had spent at least an hour trying things on, dithering because she needed to get this right. It was tricky because she did not want to look too businesslike but nor did she want to look too glamorous. Unfortunately, Brian had brought her to Gardner's once and, mortifyingly, had refused to leave a tip so she hoped to God that they did not have the same waiter who might remember her as part of the tight-arsed couple and have her on some sort of blacklist.

Even so, with luck he might not recognize her because the last time she was here was before the drastic hair trim and she looked a little different now. Since then it had grown a bit although it was at that awkward, neither here or there 'stage', looking a little ragged round the edges, and she was tempted to have it cut off again. After the comical dressing and un-dressing session in front of her bedroom mirror, she had settled eventually on a simple knee-length blue dress with long sleeves, an all-rounder that was supposed to see you from office to evening with just a clever switch of accessories and although it was chilly in the evening air she was wearing just a featherweight cream fringed stole over it because her winter coat looked silly. A pair of her highest heels completed the outfit because Daniel still topped her in height terms and her only jewellery was the silver drop earrings that her parents had bought her for Christmas.

Daniel was wearing a suit – Marcus would be pleased – and a subtly striped shirt with the silk tie she and Janet had bought him for Christmas. That was a nice touch and it made her feel guilty because she had ditched his gift of the 'Bella-Sophia' perfume and reverted to her perennial favourite, a light, flowery fragrance. She was confident that such a subtlety would not occur to Daniel and that, in the unlikely event it did, he would be far too polite to mention it.

'Good evening, sir, madam.' Hell, it was the same waiter but he thankfully gave no sign of remembering her as he showed them to a corner table in the softly glowing restaurant. The menus – a vast selection of delights – were flourished and he left them in peace saying that the wine waiter would be with them shortly.

'Well … here we are.' Daniel looked at her and it occurred that they had never before been in such close proximity or if they had it would have been across a desk with piles of paperwork spread out between them and a deadline looming. It could be the lighting this evening, this being so much kinder to the eye than office fluorescent, but it was as if she was seeing him properly for the very first time and it was disconcerting; the first time she supposed that she was looking at him as a man rather than the boss.

'This is very nice, Daniel. Quite a treat.'

'You deserve it. You've worked your socks off lately, especially since Christmas.'

'Thanks. It's helped to take my mind off things.'

She found she was surprisingly flustered by the way he was looking at her, knowing that her make-up was already losing its edge and in the cool of this air-conditioned interior, the stole was useless and slippery as an eel. Irritated with it, she draped it over the back of the chair where it hung a moment before sliding gracefully off onto the carpet, lying there in a surprisingly large silky puddle. Reaching quickly down to collect it before it tripped up some unsuspecting waiter she stuffed it under the table beside her bag, fumbling a bit because, during the sitting down ceremony – waiter respectfully assisting – the bag had somehow got its strap caught round the leg of her chair. When she surfaced at last she saw that Daniel was regarding her with a bemused smile, forcing a rueful response.

'Sorry. I'm afraid I don't do accessories and I don't do elegance, either.'

'You look lovely,' he told her. 'We're not in the office now, Amy, so do try to relax. Have you decided what you would like?'

'I'll have the spiced parsnip soup and then the sea bass,' she told him, never one to dally where food was concerned. Menus these days were akin to reading *War and Peace* and she had learned how to skim them.

'Okay. Let's order then.'

The waiter had been standing at a discreet distance and approached as he saw that they had made their choices. They ordered and Daniel asked for the wine list and after consulting her – sweet of him but she didn't know one wine from another – he ordered a bottle of an Australian white, not the cheapest on the list, as she quickly noted.

'Have you been to Australia?' he asked when they were alone once more.

'No. I'd love to go but apart from anything else it's finding the time and the money for a holiday like that. Have you?' she asked, sensing a conversation opener was being offered. She was incredibly nervous because she wanted this evening to go well, even if it was just business on his part although the 'You look lovely,' had registered as had the look on his face when he said it. My God, he meant it.

'Yes, I've been several times. My ex wife was … is … Australian,' he said softly. 'She went back home after the divorce.'

'I see.' A vision of an attractive healthy-looking blonde appeared but she was glad that no name had been mentioned. 'Do you have children?'

'No. She didn't want children. She was far too busy with her career,' he added with a knowing glance her way. 'Like a lot of you ladies these days.'

'Chance would be a fine thing,' she said lightly, not taking offence to that remark when she might well have because the assumptions people made about women who had a career were laughable and often completely off track. 'I never set out to have children but it might have been different if I'd met the right man. Who knows? Now, it's getting a bit late because I'm on the slippery slope to forty.'

'Am I supposed to say you don't look it?' His grin was unrepentant and she laughed.

'You can if you like. Sometimes, lately, I've felt about eighty. However … ' she shook her head as she thought about it, 'I'm happy with what I'm doing and I refuse to think of what might have been. What's the point of that? If it happens, it happens; if it doesn't, it doesn't.'

'That's the right way to think about life,' he said, surprisingly serious but then it was him who had brought up the subject of his ex-wife. 'You have to know when it's time to end a relationship and that's what happened to us. It was difficult as these things are and we said we should remain friends but we've lost touch and that's how it should be. It's easier because she's on the other side of the world and she's met somebody else at that.'

'That's good, isn't it? It means that she's moving on and … ' she hesitated, not sure what she was trying to say, relieved, therefore, when he stepped in.

'I was at a loose end for a while and I did think of following her, another part of Australia, of course, but it's not for me. I'm not your outdoor type so all that sun and surfing doesn't appeal.'

'Nor me,' she said with a shudder. 'I'm terrified of the sea. My mother says I was frightened when I was a baby. She used to take me to these swimming classes and this particular teacher was a bit gung-ho, insisting that if babies were thrown in at the deep end, so to speak, they would just swim naturally.'

He grimaced. 'Sounds bad. Don't tell me she did it literally.'

'According to Mum,' she smiled. 'It might be hugely exaggerated and it probably is but it's true that I've hated the water ever since. And I definitely don't care for too much sun or all those scary insects so Australia is probably not for me, either.'

'Their wine is fantastic, though,' he said, pausing as their starters arrived. His was a caramelized apple salad, beautifully presented as an edible still-life and her small bowl of soup was decorated with a swirl of minted yoghurt.

'What about those speeches this afternoon?' he said as they started to eat.

'Yours was good. Very succinct,' she said.

'I've come to know what people expect. Mr Armitage knows that, too. Poor Beatrice, though. She was worried sick about having to speak in public.'

'She told me that. I'm surprised because she seems so self-assured and she must have done it before. The last thing you expect is for a woman like her to be nervous.'

'Appearances can be deceptive. She did well, though, didn't she, even if it was a touch over the top?'

Amy concentrated on her soup, feeling it would be unwise to criticise Bea – or Beatrice as he seemed to prefer. She was dying to find out his take on the Bea situation and find out exactly what, if anything, had gone on between them but how could she? This was supposed to be a business meeting but it didn't feel like it at the moment, not with his eyes on her every time she glanced up; a distinctly admiring glance at that as her womanly instinct told her.

Daniel was looking relaxed. She had always thought him handsome but here, in such cosy proximity, she was taking in every inch of his face in quick surreptitious glances. It was obvious he had had a close shave shortly before he picked her up, which said something because often he had appeared at work with that designer stubble look and she thought of him maybe trying out a few of his own outfits before choosing the formality of a suit, shirt and tie.

Surely he wasn't trying to impress her?

A warm feeling began to encircle her and as their starters were removed and they waited for their main courses, it occurred with a dreadful certainty that she was well on the way to falling in love with him. In fact, could it be that she had known all along but had refused to allow herself to think it whilst they were colleagues because she was far too professional to fall for all that?

Daniel Coleridge was all she wanted in a man: kind, thoughtful, generous and most important of all she was starting to fancy him like crazy, starting to imagine what it would be like to have him kiss her, hold her, make love to her. But how could she possibly compete with the glossy glamour of Bea who no doubt would wear slinky silk to bed rather than M&S long-sleeved cotton T-shirts? She recalled her dream where Bea had worn old pyjamas, her face scraped clean of make-up, but that was just a dream although she did wonder if Daniel had ever seen that lovely lady with a scrubbed face.

'I was going to set up base in Manchester,' he began, looking at her directly and she realized that the business part of this was about to start so she would be wise to stop all this drooling nonsense and sit up and take notice. 'I chose Manchester only because I know it well and a friend offered me a small office and a flat to go with it. But I've decided to operate from Preston, which is your neck of the woods. I went over there and I was impressed by it. It's a dynamic place, just off the M6 and I've got contacts there.' He fished a card from his pocket. 'There you go.'

'Thanks.' She left the card on the table, not wanting to risk another dive under it to her still firmly anchored bag. 'I've decided not to take the job in Preston even if I'm offered it,' she said. 'And I'm not staying here, either. But what I have decided is to step up, do my duty and take charge of the family business. My brother is going to live in France and although my mother is very capable, she needs help.'

'So you'll be moving back home?'

Was it her imagination or did he seem pleased?

'That's the idea although I haven't spoken to my mother about it yet. The house is huge and she's all on her own so I hope she'll be glad of the company.'

Their main courses arrived and there was the usual flourish as the plates were placed in front of them. They admired the look of them, making approving noises before resuming their conversation.

'I feel I have to do it,' Amy continued. 'My father always expected me to go into the business, trained me up for it and I let him down by not following through. He never said as much but my mother made it quite clear how disappointed she was. And so my brother stepped in but his heart was never in it and now that he's going I have no alternative. My mother could sell it on, of course, but it's been in the family for generations and I certainly don't want to be the one who gives up on it. It's purely my decision. She hasn't put any pressure on me.'

'That sounds very commendable but it's a bit of a blow to me. The point of all this ...' he gestured round the room, '... the point was to ask you to come and work for me, to work *with* me, rather. But obviously you have to do what you have to do so I wish you well. We'd have made a good team, though, you and me. I've already got a list of small businesses who have asked for help. There's a lot of soul searching going on out there and a lot of people worried about the future. At least I want to help them to see the options.'

'So, you want me to work with you?'

'Yes. Don't look so surprised. As I've said before, we make a good team, you and I, and I love the way we bounce ideas off each other.'

Amy put down her fork. So this was indeed the sole purpose of this evening and she had grossly misinterpreted his true intentions. This evening was purely business and she was allowing her imagination to run riot to read anything more into it.

She resumed eating, even though suddenly it was as if she was eating sawdust, only half taking in what he was saying and desperately wanting this to be over. One thing was sure. She could never work with him again.

'I've been beavering a bit behind the scenes since before Christmas,' he said. 'I've done some research into whether or not there was a need for this service because I didn't want to go into it half-arsed, if you'll excuse the expression. As it is, it's a gamble but one worth taking. If it fails – and I don't think it will – then I can go back into the big-store scenario but I think I shall like working with people, enterprising people like your father.'

'I don't think we shall be calling on you,' she said before he might suggest it. 'I've been thinking about things and have come up with a few ideas to bring us up to scratch. I think Dad lost his edge a little and following his illness earlier last year things slipped.'

Daniel did not answer immediately, taking a sip of his wine and inquiring after her choice of main.

'It's delicious. And I'm sorry to turn down your offer of a job especially when I'm having such a lovely time.'

'Are you, Amy?' There was a wistful note in his voice and she looked up sharply.

'What is it with you and Bea?' she asked throwing caution

to the wind. 'You talk about her a lot.'

'Do I?' He seemed astonished. 'I wasn't aware of it. There's nothing going on as such. I mean, we went out a couple of times before Christmas, had lunch together and so on but it tailed off. It was a mutual decision and we hadn't got as far as having a relationship as such. Why? What has she been saying?'

'Just that she likes you and she's sad you're leaving.'

'I like her, too. She's a very nice woman once you get your head around that theatrical look.'

Amy laughed. 'That "theatrical" look as you put it is meant to look natural and it costs a fortune. But I think I know what you mean. That's why I don't bother with make-up, not much, anyway,' she said, hoping that didn't sound as if she was fishing for a compliment for the second time tonight.

Luckily it passed him by. She paused, watching as he poured more wine into their glasses, not giving the hovering waiter a chance to top them up.

'Perhaps we'll catch up then when you move to Preston?'

'That would be nice.'

She half expected him to bring out his diary to fix up something definite because the 'perhaps' was altogether too vague for her liking but he did not and she most certainly was not going to tie him to a date herself.

The rest of the meal passed pleasantly and she duly noted the lavish cash tip he left. Afterwards he dropped her off at home and she chose not to ask him in because she did not want him to get any ideas; after all he had made it plain that the point of the dinner had been for him to offer her a job, which she had declined.

'You've got my card,' he said as he pulled the car to a halt. 'Give me a call when you get over there.'

'Will do.' She hoped he wasn't going to do the gentlemanly thing and escort her to the door because then there would be that awkward moment when they had to decide whether or not a goodnight kiss would be appropriate.

God, how old was she? And he was hardly your spotty teenage boy, either.

To her relief, he just smiled and nodded his goodbye from the driver's seat. She then spoilt what was meant to be a dignified exit from his life by struggling to open the car door, so that he was forced to lean over her to direct her towards the right lever. She caught a whiff of cologne, something nice, shocked by how she felt at that sudden incredible nearness.

He noticed her scent too, freshly applied before she exited the restaurant, and commented on it, saying that she smelled gorgeous but then rather spoiling it by adding that Beatrice was right and it was a lovely perfume.

It was not worth correcting him although the mention of Bea – yet again – was not welcome. If there was nothing going on then why on earth did he keep going on about the wretched woman?

'Bye then, Daniel,' she said. 'Good luck with everything and thanks for the meal.'

'Thanks for coming along. It was great. And good luck with your business, too. If you need any help you know who to call.'

He waited, engine at the ready, until she found her key and opened the door and then he drove off.

Slowly and feeling incredibly frustrated she went up the stairs to her flat.

Chapter Sixteen

Monique's phone had miraculously started working again next morning and she managed to get through to Mike just before he set off in search of her.

'I was worried sick,' he said. 'And Mum is tearing her hair out. She thought you had been kidnapped or raped or murdered. I knew you'd be fine, sweetheart, but I wish now I hadn't let you go on your own. I'm not going to let you do that ever again.'

'Aren't you, now? I can look after myself, Mike, but it's nice that you care.'

'Of course I care. I told you I was worried sick. I don't know what I'd do without you. I love you.'

It was a surprising admission coming over the phone and she said she loved him, too, which she suddenly realized she did; his voice across the miles was such a comfort.

'Don't come over yet,' she told him having already decided not to mention the state of the cottage to him. 'I'm going to stay with Aunt Sylvie for a few days before I come back. She wants to spend some time with me. Is that okay with you?'

'Of course. Stay as long as you like. Was the cottage nice?'

'Fine. Look, I'm sorry I have to go. Speak to you soon. Bye, darling.'

'I love you,' he repeated and she felt her eyes mist up. Good heavens, twice in as many minutes.

She felt curiously bereft as she ended the call. Her aunt had suggested they meet somewhere and then Sylvie would drive them the rest of the way in her car because she was hopeless at giving directions and driving in Paris was a nightmare that she was not going to inflict on her *beloved* niece. When Monique was ready to return she would drive her back to where she had left her car and Monique could then easily find her way home.

The arrangement was a little complicated but that was the plan although lately Monique had come to realize that making too many plans was a grave mistake. Her own plans for an idyllic life in an idyllic village in France had taken a hammering these past few days.

'I'm very disappointed in the cottage. It's falling to bits,' she said towards the end of their phone conversation. 'Did you know?'

'We'll talk about that later,' her aunt said airily. 'Drive carefully.'

Monique drove to the rendezvous without difficulty, parking in a narrow side street just off the town square and hoping that it would be safe to leave her car there for the next few days without getting a parking ticket. She walked through the little market, its stalls full of gorgeous-looking fruit and flowers, smelling divine, and on a sudden impulse she bought herself a fresh peach and bit at once into the plump flesh, the juice running down her chin.

Big mistake. The last thing she wanted was to drip peach juice down her front. She stepped to the side, against a wall, to finish it off carefully before finding a tissue and dabbing at her mouth.

Knowing she would be assessed in an instant by her chic aunt, she had dressed with care this morning, looking out of the window of the hotel first thing and seeing a perfect blue sky. She was wearing a dress that Christine had bought her for her last birthday. It was a Laura Ashley label, dated late sixties, a very demure floral cotton dress, the bodice diagonally tucked with long sleeves and lace-edged cuffs. She had taken time with her hair, tying it back into a high plait and she was quick to notice sly glances from a few Frenchmen as she made her way through the market. Did she look French? She rather hoped she did.

Aunt Sylvie still managed to subtly out do her, though. She was dressed in a scarlet silk two-piece, nipped in at the waist with a broad black leather belt. As they embraced, she suggested they have a coffee and a cake sitting outside the café under one of the striped parasols.

'It's like summer already,' Monique said as they sat down and Sylvie briskly ordered.

'It's the fickle season. We shall have rain tomorrow,' Sylvie said with a smile. 'You look charming, my angel. Only the very young can wear something like that.'

Feeling the comment was a slight put down – after all she was not *that* young – Monique smiled nonetheless, for she didn't want to get this off to a bad start.

'The cottage is a wreck,' she began as they waited for the coffee to arrive. 'I wasn't exaggerating when I said it's falling to bits. The shutters are hanging off and you can see right through the roof and the rain has been coming in the bedroom and there's damp everywhere; it's just awful. There was something scurrying about in the kitchen,' she added with a shudder. 'If we were in England there would be squatters in.'

'Squatters?' she frowned. 'I'm sorry but I don't know that word.'

Monique waved a hand, not wanting to explain. 'It looks nothing like the cottage in that photograph you gave me.'

'You do surprise me.' She did not look the least surprised. 'Madame Perret assured me recently that all was well.'

'She was lying.'

Sylvie looked at her sharply. 'How dare you suggest such a thing?'

Monique flinched at the rebuke, recalling suddenly that when she was little she had often been delivered similar ones by this lady opposite. It was a sad but inescapable fact that nobody in her family really liked children and although she was never physically ill-treated, she was virtually ignored. Cuddles had been thin on the ground.

The rebuke coming now very nearly caused her to utter an apology but she held her tongue as her aunt continued, face grim. 'I don't like your tone. I hope you're not blaming me, Monique. I have regular reports from Madame Perret and was under the impression that all was well. Perhaps you were tired and not seeing the potential of it. Houses can be fixed. And it is yours for free. I am giving it to you as a token of good faith.' The shrug signified that she didn't know what she was making all this fuss about.

Their coffee arrived accompanied by the two *tartelettes* that Sylvie had ordered; delicious-looking confections, one of sliced peaches, almonds and hazelnut cream; the other lemon with buttercream rosettes, both of them a work of art.

'Which would you prefer?' Sylvie smiled at her and it would seem she was forgiven. Forgiven for speaking the truth?

'The peach one,' she said at once, taking the little pastry fork and thanking Sylvie in as gracious a manner she could manage under the circumstances. She was annoyed at her aunt's reaction, for it was obvious that she was going to wriggle out of any responsibility for the cottage, which was extremely underhand of her. How could she explain the photograph? She felt her dream and all her plans fading away and it made her feel sick. After one mouthful, she had to push the plate away.

'You look pale,' Sylvie said, changing the subject although there was no way she was going to get away with that. Things needed to be resolved. 'Are you quite well?'

'I'm pregnant,' she murmured and suddenly, saying it

aloud, made it real.

Sylvie clattered her cup on the saucer. '*Mon Dieu!* This is so unexpected. I ... ' an uncertain smile appeared. 'Have I to congratulate you?'

'No, no ... please,' Monique stopped her. 'I haven't told Mike yet.'

'Why ever not? He must be the first to know.' Her smile had broadened, seemed genuine enough. 'I am very flattered, my dear, that you should tell me before your husband but I think I understand. You do not want to give the news over the phone. Why did you not tell him before you came?' She looked at her thoughtfully. 'I see. He would perhaps have not allowed you to travel so far on your own if he knew you were expecting a child?'

'It's not that,' she said, holding a hand over her mouth as a wave of nausea reared up. Why had she blurted it out to this woman when she had not told Christine or Mike or Amy?

Or Sol?

Sylvie caught her mood. 'What is it? What is the matter? You can tell me. You are concerned, of course, about having it but I am told that it is all a big fuss about nothing. Babies are born all the time and when you see some of the women who have them then it can't be *that* difficult.'

She shook her head. 'It's not that. If only it were that.'

There was a silence and she watched a couple at a nearby table, young and in love, wondering for a moment if she and Mike had ever looked like that.

'You are afraid to tell him and that can mean only one thing.' Sylvie was now speaking softly for her ears only. Around them, the townsfolk were enjoying the sunshine and the place was bustling. Monique listened to excited French voices and from an open window music blared out. A young woman passed by on a bicycle – smiling and cheerfully relaxed and going against all the rules on health and safety – with a flowing skirt that could catch in the wheel, a gossamer scarf that would provide no protection if she fell off and to top it all, a tiny child sitting in a basket arrangement behind her.

'That would be frowned upon in England; it's dangerous,' she said and her aunt frowned, too, but not at the woman on the bike and, as they looked at each other there was no need to spell it out because Aunt Sylvie had already guessed.

'I thought you might have a lover, Monique, and you are afraid to tell your husband because you fear the baby is not his,' she said. It was a statement not a question.

Amy appeared with a dog in her arms.

'Meet Oscar,' she said, putting him down in the hall. 'Don't worry, he's house trained. I got him from the dog's home. Poor darling, he's been moved from pillar to post this last year so we'd better make sure he stays put here.'

'You never mentioned a dog.' Christine looked at the creature who was now sitting in the hall looking at her inquiringly. They used to have a dog, years ago, when the children were small but after he passed on they had somehow never got round to getting another. There had been brief further forays into animal ownership with the children wanting a guinea pig, a short-lived affair, followed by a cat who had wandered off one day never to return and lately, for the last few years, nothing at all. 'You might have said, Amy. You can't just turn up on the doorstep with a dog.'

'Look at him. Isn't he just adorable?'

They looked at him. He was brown and white and some sort of spaniel cross, according to the kennels. Also, according to the kennels he ticked various boxes; good with children, good with cats, affectionate. He was four years old and in need of a home and, after the impulsive visit to the kennels Amy had succumbed to his charm.

'I can't take him back. Please, Mum, don't make me take him back,' Amy said, sounding about six years old again.

'He's been ever so good and it was no picnic having him in the flat. He'll love living here with all the open space.'

Christine was wavering. Why not? She would have had another dog after they lost theirs but it was Frank who put his foot down. 'Whose dog is it?' she asked. 'Is it yours or mine?'

'Both of ours. I'll be living here too, remember.'

'But perhaps not forever. We need to be sure about this, darling. We can't just take on a responsibility like this without giving it a lot of thought.' She looked at the dog, who was still sitting but with his head now cocked. 'Suppose you get married and move? What then? Will you take the dog or leave him with me?'

'Mum! You're creating difficulties when they haven't yet arisen. We shan't be fighting a custody battle if that's what you're saying. Oscar can stay here if – and it's a big if – I ever get married and leave. I'm here to help with the business so I can't see a problem for the foreseeable future.'

'Who's going to walk him?'

Oscar pricked up his ears and stood up, his tail beginning a slow uncertain wag.

'We aren't going to argue about that, are we? Look, can I get my stuff inside? Andy's waiting in the van.'

'All right.' Christine bent down and fussed the dog, running her hands over his silky coat, looking into those big brown eyes and knowing that the deed was done. Oscar was staying put. Already she was contemplating a trip into town to get various things for him and she would make a special doggy corner for him in the utility room. He would soon know his place.

'I know he won't replace Dad,' Amy said quietly. 'How daft. But he will help a bit.'

There in the hall with Andy still patiently waiting outside, they gave each other a hug, Christine feeling the slight tremble of Amy's body against her. She wanted to say something, to try to explain just why she had been so disappointed all those years ago. She had wanted a boy first time around and Amy had turned out to be a girl, and a daddy's girl at that. That initial disappointment had lodged inside and she saw now that she had never given her a chance. She had never quite forgiven her daughter, either, for the childhood accident that had scarred Mike for life. She had never seen so much blood and she still recalled that anxious trip to A&E carrying him in her arms and dragging a sobbing Amy along with her.

It was an accident but it was Frank who swept up the little girl in his arms when they arrived home fussing *her* instead of the wounded soldier. Holding Amy in her arms now, comforting her, she wanted to say something, to try to offer an explanation but there was no need. Amy knew exactly what was what but she smiled as they gently disengaged themselves.

'Best start unloading or we'll be here all bloody day.'

They jumped as they heard Andy's cheery voice – big burly heavily tattooed Andy who took no prisoners – and went outside. Christine quickly saw that Amy had brought along a lot of boxes, stuff that had sat for a long time up in the loft at Snape House, most of which was probably destined to go up there again, moveable rubbish, most of it.

Oscar wandered outside with them. He looked very happy as he set off to explore the garden, busily making his mark everywhere. After they had finished unloading the van, Christine put the kettle on. She was not in the removal business for nothing and she knew that, once that van was empty the next thing on the agenda was a cup of tea.

Chapter Seventeen

'Monique's staying at her aunt's in Paris for a few days,' Mike informed them.

He had come over to see Oscar and Amy – in that order – and had enthused over one of them. He had taken the news that Amy had resigned from her job and was moving into Snape House badly, even though Amy felt he should be bloody glad that she was going to sort things out. It was all very well him coming up with all these ideas for the business, all these plans of his, but why the hell hadn't he done so before? Had he been so in awe of Dad that he hadn't dared speak his mind? Ideas had to be implemented and action had to be taken and if there was one thing she was good at, it was making decisions and taking action.

This business was in serious need of a good shake-up.

It had been one of those exceptional spring days, warmer than average, and although it was tempting to set the outdoor table and eat their meal there they had decided against it and were eating in the kitchen instead.

Christine had cooked salmon with new potatoes and a home-made sauce with some French beans and Mike was demolishing his as if he hadn't eaten in ages.

'Did you get the chance to speak to Monique for long?' Amy asked. 'What did she say about the cottage? She has been to see it, hasn't she?'

'She didn't say much. She's met up with her aunt, who

asked her to stay for a few days and she jumped at the chance.'

'I'm not surprised. I wouldn't mind a few days in Paris myself. If she plays her cards right she might get treated to some designer clothes,' Amy said, tongue in cheek because she knew damned well that most of Monique's vast wardrobe came from charitable sources, in other words, her mother and now the French aunt. She should be so lucky.

'It was a brave thing to do, driving there on her own,' Christine said, giving Amy a look she knew well. 'We mustn't forget that she lost her mother back in November,' she added and then, for Mike's benefit, 'although as nobody bothered to tell us about that we weren't able to offer any support at the time.'

'It was the way she wanted it, Mum.' Mike was standing firm on that. 'She didn't want a fuss.'

'So she deserves a little treat,' Christine continued, letting it pass. 'And I have to say that aunt of hers sounds as if she's rolling in money. She lives in this huge apartment, doesn't she Mike, right in the middle of Paris overlooking some avenue or other.'

Amy laughed. 'I'm glad I'm not relying on you, Mum, for directions.'

'It'll be nice for them to spend some time together,' Mike said defensively. 'You know that her father never bothers to contact her now that he's remarried. Poor darling. She's had a rough time. She reckons she was an unfortunate mistake and by the time her mother realized she was pregnant it was too late to do anything about it.'

'God, Mike, that's a terrible thing to say,' Amy said, genuinely shocked that he should come out with such a thing. 'I'm sure that wasn't the case,' she added although it did give her an insight into Monique's psyche and out of nowhere she felt an enormous urge to make amends for all the unpleasant things she might have said or done or thought.

'Families!' Christine said with feeling. 'That's why I've always thought of her as my own daughter because she has never really had a proper mother of her own.'

'I'm your daughter,' Amy said and it sounded mean and pathetic so she switched the conversation abruptly to the business, asking if there was anything she ought to know before she set foot in the office the following week.

'You'll find out as you go.' Mike sighed and pushed his plate aside, reaching for the jug of iced water. 'Go easy at first. They're all a bit sensitive and now that Shirley's on her way we need to keep an eye on bookings and the diary. She was good at that.'

'She was so good that nobody else could make head nor tail of her system,' Christine remarked with a short laugh.

'We shall soon change that. Have we had any feedback from clients recently? Any criticisms we should be taking on board?'

'Don't let's talk shop.' Christine started to clear up and Oscar, seeing signs of activity, got up from his basket, stretched and then went to stand beside her at the sink.

'He's taken to you, Mum,' Amy said with a smile. 'Isn't that great, Mike? Have you ever thought of getting a dog? I know that Monique likes them. Or maybe … ' she exchanged a quick glance with her mother, 'are you planning on starting a family any time soon? Shoot me if that's too personal but it would help us if we knew.'

'We would love a family,' he said, cheeks flushing. 'But it's not—'

'Ah. Sorry, I didn't mean to pry,' she interrupted hastily, knowing at once what he was *not* saying. My goodness, they were having problems, which was a surprise considering Monique's comparatively tender years.

There was a short silence, Amy busying herself with collecting up the dishes and carrying them over to the sink. Her mother rarely bothered to use the dishwasher, which sat there still in sparkling condition. She said that she liked washing up by hand because it gave her the opportunity to stare out at the garden and work out what needed doing.

'Has Monique seen a doctor?' Christine was more forthcoming now that the delicate subject had been broached. 'Have *you*?'

'No I have not. For God's sake, Mum.' He stood up and collected the remainder of the items on the table and they both knew him better than to pursue it. Men were sensitive about issues like that but Amy knew that, now it was out in the open, Christine would be quizzing Monique when she got back.

After they had eaten, it was still fairly light and Christine took Oscar out for a walk down to the village. It was an entirely different ballgame having a walk accompanied by a dog. He was a friendly soul and had already acquired a group of doggy friends, which meant that Christine was making new friends too. Aside from the ladies from church who were more acquaintances than real friends she realized that if she was to make a new start, making friends was the way to go about it. Oscar was the key. He was much admired and it amused her that doggy people said hello to Oscar before they did her.

'My daughter's come back home,' she told the owner of a black poodle, both of whom seemed enamoured of Oscar at first sight.

'That will be lovely for you.' The dog's owner smiled a consoling smile. 'It'll help take your mind off things.'

She had heard that expression often recently and was not sure what it meant exactly. If it meant that it would help her forget Frank, how was that possible when he was still around in the house? Not physically around, of course, but, even though Mike had cleared all his stuff away, taking it goodness knows where, there was still so much to remind her of him.

The poodle lady whose name she had already forgotten

had meant well and Christine vowed to take on a more active role in her little community. Just how long had she lived here, for heaven's sake and she could not think of a single person whom she could count as a true friend. It was hardly surprising, though, for she had been guilty of behaving like the lady of the manor, keeping her distance and not allowing anybody to get close. She'd had some friends when the children were small and she was taking and picking them up from school but, one by one, they had all moved on and for the last five years or so she had spent her spare time with Monique, which had effectively excluded her from other things.

Now was the time to change. She might even start going along to church to which somebody had already issued an invitation. 'Come and sit with me,' the lady had said, 'and afterwards we can have tea and biscuits and a natter.'

She hesitated because she found the holy silence in that place more disturbing than comforting. But she took the view that not many of the folk who attended were truly religious. They went along for different reasons and surely God, if there was one, would understand that, although she might be wise to keep quiet about her doubts. Socially, they were an active bunch and they were always raising money for some thing or another. She could help with that.

She was worried sick now after Mike had let slip that he and Monique had been trying for a baby for a while. Well, of course that would explain why Monique had been reluctant to talk too much about it and she hoped to goodness that there wasn't going to be a problem there. Hopes faded of her lovely little baby granddaughter or grandson arriving any time soon and in any case, when they went off to France she would not be seeing much of her or him anyway.

When she returned home, Amy and Mike were in the family room chatting and looking relaxed. Mike seemed to have recovered from his bout of irritation that Amy was diving headlong into the business but then what had he to grumble about? It was he who was jumping ship. Frank would have been delighted that his long-held hopes were finally coming to fruition and she just knew that Amy would quickly whip things into shape. There was a certain steely resilience about her daughter that was at once scary and impressive.

She was not to know then that Mike's plans of a new life in France were about to fall apart.

Chapter Eighteen

Amy was checking through the company records and the audited accounts. She was no accountant but it was clear that everything was in order, which was a relief because she had had a nagging feeling that Shirley had been embezzling funds for years, pulling the wool over her father's eyes with that flirtatious manner.

She was in her father's study, which they had not touched so it remained pretty much as it had always been. There was a desk with an old-fashioned in-and-out tray and a Victorian rosewood stationery box. It was a handsome masculine piece with its satinwood interior, writing slope and blotter, never used as such in today's computer age but attractive to look at. There was a big old bookcase, the books on the shelves reflecting her father's interest in the Second World War and a few indifferent pictures on the wall, probably not her father's choice but they fitted in with the green colour scheme.

Sitting at his desk in the big old swivel chair had seemed odd at first but she was getting used to it and saw no reason to change too much in this room. There was a limit to what could be done with a home office and that was how it should be. Oscar had taken to coming with her and was curled up beside her chair when her mobile rang.

'Hi, Amy, it's Daniel.'

'Daniel!' she felt her heart thud and as she lost

concentration her notes slipped off the desk and thudded onto the floor, several pages fluttering loose and landing on the surprised dog who, affronted, stood up and shook himself free of them. It was lucky Daniel couldn't see her and the effect his voice had on her. The pleasure at hearing his voice was unexpected in its intensity. She would pick the papers up in a minute. 'How are you?'

'How are you, more's the point? I've been worried about you.'

'Have you?' She was pleased about that for in order for somebody to worry about you they had to care. She had thought about him from time to time, debated calling him, in fact, but it was so much better that he was contacting her first. 'I'm absolutely fine. Never better, although, well, obviously I'm still a bit up and down,' she amended carefully. 'But I'm just about to get started on taking over the family business so it's a bit hectic just now. I'm looking through the accounts at this very moment,' she said with a laugh.

'Oh God, I'm not disturbing you, am I?'

'Not at all. My head's spinning with figures. How are things with you?'

'All right.' He sounded cautious. 'It takes time to get these things off the ground properly but I'm being kept fairly busy and I've sent out my first few invoices.'

'Great. I've got a dog,' she told him happily, noticing suddenly that Oscar was taking an interest in the papers that had showered round him and was now in danger of seriously messing them up. 'Give me a minute,' she said, bending down to retrieve them and depositing them in a heap on the desk. The desk faced the window, a real distraction, and she could see her mother out there talking to the gardener, waving her arms about in what was bound to be a serious horticultural discussion.

'A dog? What kind?'

'A bit of this and that,' she said and then as a sudden

thought struck her. 'Do you like dogs?'

'You bet. There was always a dog around when I was little but you can't have one, can you, when you live alone and you're out all day.'

'No. It's not fair on them.'

Oscar, knowing she was talking about him, laid his head on her lap and looked up at her, pleading for a walk. Amy, running out of sensible things to say and needing to move it on from doggy matters, hesitated, relieved when he carried on.

'I've been very busy and as well as everything else I've bought myself a flat in town,' he said. 'I'd very much like you to see it sometime. How about we meet for lunch next week?'

'To talk shop?'

'Hell, no. Just to catch up, that's all. It'll be nice to see a friendly face.'

They fixed a date and this time she knew it was a genuine date. She still was not sure of his intentions, for 'friendly face' could mean just that, but she had an instinctive gut reaction that he had feelings for her every bit as she did him. She always had, she now realized, but when they worked together they had kept their distance and avoided serious eye or hand contact. It was only when they had let their guard down on that so-called business date at Gardner's that she had finally admitted to herself that, inconvenient as it might turn out to be, she had fallen for him.

'Come on, Oscar,' she said when she clicked off the phone. 'Let's go for a walk.'

He had called. He had asked her out. And this time she knew exactly where it was leading.

She took the dog up the hill, walking swiftly past the bench. The memory would always be there but it was a lovely walk and they could not avoid it for ever so she had done it several times since then. Letting Oscar off when they reached the flat top of the hill she watched as, released from the lead, he raced around. There was nobody about and frankly she felt much like doing the same thing, running round and round just for the sheer joy of it, the anticipation of what was to come very nearly overwhelming her.

She caught up with Mike a few days later at the office. He was just about to head off to do an assessment for a potential client and after annoying the lads last time because he had grossly underestimated the time a packing would take, which had shot their already tight schedule to pieces, he was keen to get it right this time. It was not entirely his fault as he felt at pains to point out to her. The difficulty, he told her, was that sometimes the client managed to find a few extra things that they 'forgot' to point out to you at the assessment, which always messed things up on the removal day itself.

'I know but we should always allow a little leeway,' she said keeping her voice light because she knew he was sensitive about it. 'Is Monique on her way back?'

'No. She's staying over a few more days,' he said, a certain wariness creeping in. 'I've told her there's no rush. She might as well stay a while longer.'

'Is everything all right with you two? There isn't a problem is there?'

'No. Should there be?' That aggression was never far off and she felt her own temper rising because she had only asked a civil question.

'It's just that I thought she would be glad to get back and tell you all about it. She must be missing you.'

'She is.' He sighed and picked up his briefcase. 'I've got to go. I'm due there at two o'clock and it's a long drive.'

'Are you happy for me to ask this Martin guy to revamp the website? It looks like nothing on earth just now. It needs to be snappier, more up to date.'

'Thanks. Are you saying I did a rubbish job?'

'No, not at all. You did a fantastic job but it's years old and I'm just saying it's tired-looking, that's all. It was a good effort so there's no need to be so damned sensitive.'

He nodded, managing a small smile. 'Sorry. Have a word with him by all means but don't do anything without consulting with me and Mum first.'

'She's given me the go-ahead. Hang on a minute.' She stopped him in his tracks. 'You're off soon and once you set foot in France you're finished here, Mike. We need to sit down and talk things through and you have to stop resenting me. I can do this. I've got a degree in business studies.'

'Degree!' he shook his head. 'And I've got bugger all, is that what you're saying?'

'No, it's not what I'm saying. Why do you have to twist everything? Stop being so childish.'

'Sensitive? Childish? You haven't got much of an opinion of me, have you?' He laughed shortly, glancing pointedly at his watch. 'You don't know what I've had to put up with these last few years. You've been out of it, Amy, swanning round those stores of yours doing whatever it is you do while I've been stuck here trying to do my best to please that old bugger who thought I was useless, paid me a crap salary and never once said thanks. He made me feel *that* high ...' he indicated with finger and thumb just how. 'And I shall never forgive the way he gave me a bollocking in front of the lads, not once but three or four times. It was humiliating and I had no option but to stand there and take it.'

'You had a choice. You could walk away.'

'It's not that easy. You can't just pack in a job out of pique. I'm not free and easy like you. I haven't got much in the way of qualifications and I've not just got myself to think about. I have Monique. I have a wife to look after.'

'She could get herself a job, a proper job that earns proper money,' Amy finally exploded, irritated by the 'free and easy' gibe. 'She's not incapable, is she? Every other woman I know has a job unless they're looking after little kids and she doesn't have any, not yet, and maybe she never will.' She stopped, horrified at what she had said. 'Look I'm sorry, I didn't mean—'

'I'm off and thanks for that. And you dare to call *me* insensitive.' He snatched at his jacket, draped it over his arm, went out and slammed the door.

Ouch.

That was a good start, she told herself, noticing that not surprisingly their raised voices had been overheard by a couple of the lads who were out in the yard sorting out the van ready for the day's job. She needed to calm down and she knew she needed to apologize for that last remark but they had had worse rows over the years and it would be forgotten if not completely forgiven in due course.

Monique's disappearance – not quite, but it was beginning to feel like that – was worrying her mother more than her. Amy imagined that Monique would be having a lovely time in Paris, shopping, sight-seeing, probably being taken out for dinner by her aunt to some wonderful restaurants. What woman wouldn't grasp that opportunity?

However she was beginning to see a tiny glimpse of a changing of attitude where her mother and Monique was concerned, a little switch away from the annoying, cloying adoration Christine had shown her daughter-in-law for years. Perhaps it was to do with Amy's return to the family fold. Or perhaps her mother was at last beginning to understand that Monique was not quite the person she liked to present to the world.

She was a much more complex character than that. Amy had known that for years and now – and not before time – it was starting to dawn on her mother, too. It was ironic, though, that just as that relationship cooled, her relationship with her sister-in-law was just now at an all-time high. Monique had been brilliant at the consolation stuff after her father had died and Amy felt that if the two of them worked at it, things could only get better.

However, worryingly, it occurred to her that maybe, now that she was back in her beloved France being looked after by her rich aunt, they might have seen the last of her.

And maybe that thought had occurred to Mike too.

The man in the bookshop was extraordinarily handsome, tall and lean with a rangy athletic build, looking as if he could run long distance without breaking sweat. She watched as he reached up effortlessly to the top shelf to pick out a book for a petite lady, his movements relaxed and graceful. Yes, that was it; there was a grace in his manner, a charm as he smiled at the little lady that reminded her of a bygone age. He was wearing pale jeans with flared, frayed hems, sandals and a white linen shirt and he looked pretty good in them. She also liked the exotic touch of a single gold earring in one shapely ear. His hair was dark and curly and there was a touch of the bad boy about him. He was the proprietor of the bookshop and his name, a little fanciful, surely, was Solomon Diamond.

The bookshop was up a side street; a busy thoroughfare between major shopping streets and you could say it was in an ideal position sandwiched between a delicatessen and a beauty salon. She must have walked past it before but had never been inside.

It was in direct competition with a charity shop further along as well as the bigger bookshop chains in town but this had a quaint feel about it. There was a musty, bookish smell as you entered and the shop was long and narrow and went back a good deal further than you would think so that you were drawn deeper into the shop to a small area at the back where you could sit down with your book and have a quick thumb through. There were two comfortable leather sofas here and a low table, a coffee machine and bottled water. Carrying a book with her Christine sat herself down, smiling at a man who was browsing through a travel book.

It was all exceedingly relaxed. There was no intrusive music blaring out and no pressure to buy and in fact Christine had already noticed that the owner seemed surprised when, roused from what looked like a catnap, he was actually being offered money for a purchase.

She recognized the voice immediately as the one on the phone and found, rather to her surprise, that it tugged at her, as had Frank's voice in the early days, having much the same 'wow' effect. She had caught this man's eye as she entered the shop, asked politely if she might browse and he had nodded and smiled such a smile that she understood what the expression weak-at-the-knees meant.

Good heavens, she found herself smiling as she was drawn deeper into the interior. She always took care with her appearance on trips to town and today she was wearing a cream jacket over a low-cut black top together with a neat pencil skirt, a style of dress she knew suited her curvy shape. She had recently had a few reddish tints put into her hair and she was wearing it up so as to show off her high cheekbones to advantage. Thank God she had no need as yet to try to hide her neck. So she knew she'd looked pretty good this morning but giving him a flirtatious glance, which she knew she was guilty of, was simply not on because she was ages older than this man and recently bereaved at that. She had no business thinking such thoughts although perhaps this was an attempt by Mother Nature to let her know that she wasn't quite finished yet.

She could still do it.

She was young enough, she supposed, to have another relationship eventually although it seemed insulting to Frank's memory to be thinking such a thing quite yet. She imagined that he would give her the go-ahead and tell her to just go for it but the chance also would be a fine thing. She had no idea why the insensitive thought had crossed her mind but it must have been seeing this man that had triggered it, for men as effortlessly good looking as him were thin on the ground.

A woman poked her head around the bookshelves, smiling at her and inviting her to help herself to a coffee.

'If you need any help, give me a shout,' she said. 'We can place an order for any of the new releases if you like and they are usually with us within a couple of days. No extra charge.'

'Thank you.'

Feeling hot and bothered Christine buried her head in the book as if her guilty thoughts were on display. Didn't they call women who fancied younger men cougars? When, just for a fleeting moment, she imagined what it might be like with a young vital body such as his she blushed inwardly at such a wicked thought.

Wrong number indeed!

She had never believed that for an instant and if he made *her* feel like this then what on earth was the effect on a pretty young woman like Monique?

Chapter Nineteen

They were in her aunt's apartment, the two long narrow windows giving views across the quiet Parisian avenue. The room was not decorated to Monique's taste being altogether too stiff and formal with its lacquered side cabinets, butter-cup-yellow silk swags above the windows and two enormous pale grey sofas sitting either side of a painted Oriental coffee table. The Asian influence must have come from Sylvie's first husband whom Monique recalled had been a Singapore business man.

Opposite her, Sylvie was relaxed in wide-legged satin trousers and a matching draped top. 'I know just the man,' she said. 'He is an old friend and very discreet. It will cost money, of course, but what does that matter? I am more than happy to help out. We can think of an excuse to explain your absence for a while because you may not feel up to travelling soon after.'

'Soon after what?' Monique was tired, ready for bed and struggling to make sense of all this. They had said very little on the way to Paris and once they approached the city she let Sylvie concentrate because the traffic was horrendous. She was very glad she was spared driving but her aunt gave as good as she got, accelerating alarmingly and crunching through the gears, gesticulating and nearly coming to blows with a taxi driver who cut her up in the middle of some fantastically complicated junction. For a moment, fearing the worst, Monique had closed her eyes.

Now they were safely installed in Sylvie's palatial apartment and her aunt was surely suggesting an abortion?

'Don't look so shocked. You have little choice, my girl. Even if you have the slightest doubt then you cannot expect your husband to be a father to a child who may not be his. It is unfair of you to put him in that position.'

'You're wrong. I *do* have a choice. I've been thinking about what to do for the last two months.'

'You must ask yourself if you want a child.' Sylvie's face was set. 'I don't believe you do. If that was what you wanted then I'm prepared to be happy for you but you don't look like a contented woman. You are so like me; I never wanted a baby, either.'

'Nor did my mother,' she said bitterly.

'Perhaps not but she made the best of it.'

Monique gave a little snort but what was the point of dragging all that up again. She looked across at her aunt who was sitting with her legs crossed, silver jewellery sparkling at throat and wrist. For a moment they were silent and then Sylvie seemed to reach a decision, leaning forward and speaking low. 'I had two abortions, Monique, and I regret neither. It was not the right moment.'

'It never is.' Monique sighed hesitating briefly but then, as confessions seemed to be the order of the day, she continued. 'I was pregnant once before when I was at college but I lost it naturally. I never told my mother. I never told the father. I did not tell a soul.'

'Would you have had it?' If Sylvie was surprised she did not show it.

'I don't know. I was still debating what to do when I miscarried.'

'Then you probably would have had it, silly girl. We can keep secrets, the two of us. You must make a decision, Monique, and quickly. It makes sense to have the procedure done here in the next few days. You can rest afterwards and I will get somebody in to take care of you. Then when you feel up to it you can return home and nobody will be any the wiser and when you are ready you can come back with your husband to live here in France and—'

'No. I don't want to live in that place,' Monique said firmly. 'I don't care if the cottage is done up and looks beautiful, it's in the wrong place. I could never settle there. I hate that village.'

'Ah.' Her aunt reached forward and took a cigarette from a silver case. 'I thought it was just me but you feel the same and so did your mother, which is why she never wanted to live there, either. I told you, the three of us have a lot in common. There were strange happenings in that village many years ago, things they are reluctant to talk about, and I don't believe it has ever recovered.'

'What sort of happenings? A serial killer on the loose?' Monique managed an uncertain laugh.

Sylvie dismissed it with a wave of her hand. 'Not that; something much more sinister, which I am not going to discuss with you. I hoped you might not notice but you are sensitive to auras as I am, as we all are in this family. It is a pity but I gave you the chance.'

'Your conscience is clear.' Monique said dryly, watching as her aunt lit the cigarette and inhaled. 'Smoking is very bad for you.'

'The good things in life are always bad for you,' Sylvie said. 'What are you going to do about this other man?'

'Finish it.'

'Are you quite sure?'

She nodded. 'I don't know what got into me, Sylvie. I love Mike and I'm mad to risk losing him.'

'I will ring my good friend in a moment,' Sylvie blew smoke heavenwards. 'The procedure can be arranged for tomorrow. The sooner the better.'

'The "procedure"? Is it legal?'

'He is a good friend,' her aunt reiterated as if that answered the question. 'And he owes me a favour.'

Daniel called to rearrange the date, putting it forward by one day and asking if she wanted to drive over and meet him at his flat before they went to dinner. It seemed perfectly sensible to do that and she did not suspect for a moment that he had an ulterior motive and would try to ravage her immediately she was through the door.

Daniel was the last man to do something like that. She did know, however, where this was inevitably leading and if she wanted she could end it anytime she liked before it got more complicated but she did not want that. She wanted to take a chance on this and see where it led because this time, so far, there were no doubts whatsoever. She did not, however, want to tempt fate by telling her mother too much about it and thank God there was no Janet now giving her knowing looks. If Janet knew what was happening she would be turning cartwheels.

It was a lovely day but then it was turning out to be one of those springs where everything was turned upside down by unseasonably warm weather. They were all being lulled into thinking that this was it for the rest of the summer when in all probability June would not be bursting out all over but would come in with a drop in temperature and blankets of cloud that wouldn't clear until August.

Amy smiled at such a pessimistic thought.

She knew the city well but there had been a lot of changes over the years and she was unfamiliar with the new traffic layout. But she wasn't too worried because she had once driven a furniture van through these streets and if she could do that she could do anything.

Daniel's flat was in the former Docks area and as she waited for him to buzz her in at the communal entrance she half expected to see a replica of Brian's place. She didn't often think of Brian these days, regarding the whole episode as a near miss, for if she had had time to consider it she might have forgiven him all sorts and compromised all ends up and as a result made the biggest mistake of her life.

The interior of the flat was, to her relief, nothing like Brian's converted barn. Daniel's sitting room, although furnished in a contemporary fashion, was so much warmer with a huge sofa and armchair covered in aubergine velvet, one wall papered in a striking silver and navy design; it was clean, uncluttered but comfortable at the same time. Yes, she approved and said as much. All it needed was a few feminine touches to lift it.

'Glad you like it,' he said, his pride evident. 'I always used to leave things to Jenny but it was good this time to have a go myself.'

So her name was Jenny. She wished he hadn't said that but it came easily to him and she knew without asking that he was well and truly over her. She wandered over to the window with its view of the renovated dock area as he went into the kitchen to make them a cup of coffee. He had bought, not rented, so that meant, presumably, that he was serious about staying here.

'Have you checked out the department stores?' she asked, wincing even as she said it because talking shop was not meant to be on her agenda this evening.

'No.' His voice from the kitchen was accompanied by the sound of cups being taken out of cupboards. 'I've been too busy and I avoid them if I can. You know me, I can guarantee I'll see things that are not quite right and it's not my job to do anything about it any more.'

She joined him in the kitchen, superbly equipped in a glossy way, a gadget-heaven far removed from the country-style kitchen at Snape House, which she much preferred.

'I know what you mean. I don't do department stores, either. This is nice, Daniel,' she said.

'What is? This flat or us being here together?'

'Both,' she said with an uncertain smile. She knew that

sooner or later one of them would make a move and considering how long they had known each other this whole tiptoeing round the real issue was faintly ridiculous. It was the twenty-first century for heaven's sake and people didn't do the courtship thing anymore, which on many levels, she thought, was a pity. Hadn't she felt that it had all happened much too quickly with Brian and look where that had ended up?

On the contrary, she felt she knew this man and yet in so many ways she did not.

'I was hoping you would get back in touch,' she said, passing him an opportunity to explain why he had.

'Sorry it wasn't earlier but I needed to think about things,' he said as he led the way back into the sitting room. She noticed a few photographs in modern frames grouped together on a small side table and he told her who was who as she glanced at them. There was no picture, she was glad to see, of the aforementioned Jenny, which was hardly a surprise but there were photos of a happy smiling group of his immediate relatives; his mum and dad, a brother and sister. 'We get on quite well,' he said with some surprise. 'We're all scattered but we do try to see each other when we can.'

'At least you don't work together,' she told him with a smile. 'That's hell. Mike is still reluctant to let go and doesn't quite trust me to do the job properly.'

Daniel laughed at that. 'He obviously hasn't heard of your reputation.'

'Which is?' she asked briskly.

'Don't get huffy.' He smiled that smile of his. 'You're known to be a tough cookie and not the sort to stand any nonsense. People respect you for that and they trust you.'

'Thank you very much.' She shook her head. 'I'm not sure I want to be known as tough. I'm not remotely tough, Daniel ... ' she added ruefully, for in an odd way it hurt to be called that. Goodness, she had felt anything but tough during these last difficult months but then again if you kept your emotions hidden then they remained just that – hidden. She had to be strong for her mother, who she knew had private little weeps, but there was nobody being strong for *her* and she needed there to be. She started to speak again, trying to explain, but she couldn't get the words out and damn it, she knew that she was in grave danger of bursting into tears. How long would this go on? She needed to snap out of it.

Daniel cottoned on in an instant but then they had always been able to read each other's minds.

'Hey, come on, I didn't mean to upset you,' he said, moving swiftly towards her and taking her in his arms. 'That's the last thing I want to do. I know how it's been for you and believe me ... ' he took a moment to draw back so that he could look at her. 'I've watched you and I've wanted to help but I didn't seem to be able to. Janet said it was best to leave you to it because you had to get through it yourself.'

'She was wrong. I needed somebody outside the family,' she said softly, falling against him once more and savouring it. 'Oh Daniel, it's been just awful. I still can't believe it happened like that.'

'I know.'

They were so close, catching each other's breath, that a kiss was inevitable and gentle at first but quickly became something else and that was enough for all the pent-up emotion of the last weeks to surface at last. She wanted to cry, she wanted to smile, but most of all she wanted him to help her through the worst of it. It felt as if she had, without realizing it, built a barrier around herself since her father's death and she needed to break through it but she could not do it by herself.

She needed him.

'Should we cancel the restaurant booking?' she said, remembering and feeling guilty. 'We should let them know,' she added. 'They might want to re-book the table.'

'Sod the restaurant,' he said, intent on what he was doing and so that evening, unsurprisingly, they never made it to the restaurant but they did make it to bed. There were no doubts this time and she knew he loved her even before he said so and she had no hesitation at all in saying that she loved him, too.

Monique was having grave doubts about going through with the 'procedure', a term that sounded much better than 'abortion'. It was surely the sensible thing to do given the circumstances but when it came to it she was hesitant.

She had been living in some sort of fairy tale these past few days, the lovely sunny weather helping and making her feel that she could live here forever under a cloudless sky. The short burst of torrential rain that had accompanied her visit to the cottage seemed appropriate now as a means of getting through to her that it would not always be like that.

Today it was grey outside. It had rained overnight and the streets were glistening and the traffic had started up with much hooting. People rarely sounded the horn in England, she realized, and when they did it was for the right reason. Why had she ever imagined herself to be French when it was obvious to all and sundry that she was as English as roast beef?

Lying on the bed, bigger than hers at home, she looked round the cold classy interior of the guest bedroom in her aunt's apartment and thought what a cold classy family she came from. On her mother's side she could trace her roots back to some aristocratic family and her mother had liked reminding them of that. Her mother had always thought herself better than anybody else, looking down on people, thinking she was a cut above, and although she grumbled later Monique did not think she was too concerned when her career in fashion journalism faltered and fizzled out when Monique came inconveniently along. She had never wanted to make the move to the north of England with her father but he was a force to be reckoned with in academic circles, a historian of repute, although his frequent affairs belied that stuffy image. Her mother had amused herself, making frequent trips to London where she had 'friends' and leaving the two of them to fend for themselves. Her father palmed her off on a selection of au pairs, never making any secret of the fact that he viewed her continued presence as a necessary nuisance.

Her Aunt Sylvie had always moved in illustrious circles and so far as Monique could see had never had a career as such, although she, too, thought of herself as artistic. Monique wondered as she grew older just why the sisters were antagonistic towards each other although perhaps her father's philandering ways were a clue to that. After one long visit, Sylvie had been effectively banished so perhaps something had gone on in the past, a bit of a fling, something that her mother did not talk about, although it may have been a contributing factor to the break up.

She was, Monique reflected, the product of two not very nice people and she worried that she would be as bad a mother herself if she chose to keep this baby.

She had no feelings towards it as yet, which was perhaps a sign that it would be history repeating itself but at the same time she did occasionally still think of the child that might have been if she had not lost it.

It was difficult to think about but it – boy or girl – would have been beautiful indeed because she and Sol were beautiful people. She was honest with herself and had no qualms in thinking such a thing for it was an undisputed fact. He was not her first man for, virtually abandoned as she was, she had tried out a few before him but it was different with Sol. Just recently she had wanted to tell him about that time when they were at college and the baby they might have had and how it had momentarily sent her into a spin but she held her tongue because what good would it do for him to know? He was a loner, not a family man, and it would have been wrong to saddle him with the memory of a child just as much as it would be wrong to trap him into a relationship now. Sol wanted it all but was not prepared to give a thing and even though she loved him she knew it was an impossible situation.

She had no reason to believe this was Sol's child; it could just as easily be Mike's for they had consoled each other a good deal following Frank's death. It might be best not to know. Babies were babies and family resemblances were often vague and with a bit of luck it might look like her. A confession just now would ruin her marriage and she now knew she did not want that. She may have married Mike for the wrong reason as her aunt suggested but that wasn't to say that she hadn't grown to love him and the thought of being without him was not one she wished to contemplate.

Outside her door, she could hear voices, Sylvie's prominent, and she knew they would come for her in a few minutes to take her to the clinic. She had no concerns that it would be safe and straightforward. It would be so simple to go through with it, to have it over with once and for all so that she would be saved the agony of seeing a child grow up, hoping against hope that it resembled her with just the barest tinge of its father. If that was the case she would get away with it. But how could she live with that hanging over her? How could she do such a thing to Mike, who was kind and caring and worth ten of Sol?

Sol Diamond – she very nearly hated him.

She heard a man's low laugh and she struggled to her feet, slipping her shoes on and sitting there a moment, heart pounding. Aunt Sylvie had gone to a lot of trouble to persuade this man to come along and it would be dreadful of her to let her down.

It was as if she was in the condemned cell and if that was the case then she had missed her last meal for she was feeling queasy today and had declined even a simple

French breakfast.

She clutched at her stomach as it heaved and suddenly, she thought of the bean-sized baby inside her and placed her hands protectively over it. If that man out there had his way then within hours it would be gone, tossed aside and forgotten. But if she went ahead she was opening up a lifetime of deception. Could she live with that? It wasn't fair to Mike, who had always treated her so well. It wasn't fair to Mike, who loved her. It was a simple procedure; she could be pregnant again soon and next time it would definitely be her husband's child.

Her mother ought to have done it too, got rid of *her,* for she had never wanted her so why had she gone through with it? If only she could see her mother one more time to talk about it, to ask her so many questions, to ask what she should do now.

A knock on the door.

'Are you ready, Monique?'

'Coming.'

There were turning points in your life and this was one of them.

She went to open it.

'It's good to have you back,' Christine said as they strolled around the garden. Something had happened in France, she knew that, but she was waiting for Monique to tell her. She did know that the cottage had been a huge disappointment, which she ought to have been delighted about but was not. She had finally realized that it was no earthly use being selfish and it would have been lovely for them, an exciting new life, if it had worked out.

'It's good to be back,' Monique said with a smile. 'I can't tell you how nice it was to see the English fields again. It sounds silly but for a while there I imagined that I was truly French when I'm not. I'm every bit as English as you and I would never have fitted in and as for Mike ... ' she laughed. 'He would have been a fish out of water. He would have hated it eventually and he would have resented me for dragging him there in the first place. His place is here running the business.'

'Yes.' Christine reached down and pulled up a weed to add to the little bag she always carried around in the garden. 'I'm thinking of moving,' she told her. 'The house is starting to get on my nerves.'

'Moving?' Monique gasped. 'But I thought they would carry you out in a box.'

'Thanks.'

'Sorry, but you know what I mean?'

'I'm not moving far,' she said quickly. 'I'm looking at a house in the village, the old post office, and I already have a potential buyer for this.'

'Have you told Amy? After all she lives here, too.'

'Not yet. But … ' Christine hesitated, 'don't say anything but I think she's serious about this man she's been seeing recently. It's her old boss, the man she worked with in Leeds and he has a flat in Preston now so I can't see that she's going to be homeless. In fact she's probably just waiting for the right moment to break it to me that she's moving in with him.'

'Will you keep Oscar?'

'Of course.' She bent down to stroke the dog that had bounded up to them from the other end of the garden. 'We can all share him.'

They sat on the bench. Monique was all in white, an ankle-length cotton skirt with a loose top, her hair in a single heavy plait. She was pale and there was an ethereal quality about her, something different.

'I'm pregnant, Christine,' she announced.

'Pregnant?' It was unexpected even though long expected and for a moment Christine was speechless. 'That's great, absolutely fantastic! What does Mike think?'

'I haven't got round to telling him yet,' she confessed,

cheeks colouring. 'Isn't it daft but I'm a bit shy about it. I want it to be the right moment and there hasn't been one since I got back. He usually asks month after month ... you know ... but he's been so busy with everything and we've had a lot to think about since I got back from France so I haven't told him.'

'Tell him tonight because I'm not going to be able to keep it a secret,' Christine said, hugging her. She felt so small and vulnerable, shaking a little under her touch and Christine, knowing the enormity of that first realization that you were carrying a child, comforted her. 'Don't worry, darling, everything will be fine.'

'I am taking a risk in having it,' Monique mumbled giving a sob against Christine's shoulder. 'It's a huge risk and I can't tell you about it.'

'Nonsense. You're young and healthy and you'll be perfectly all right. You'll have a lovely baby, you'll see.'

'Christine ...? It's not that, it's—'

'What? Is there something you want to tell me?'

Monique shifted, sniffed back tears. Christine could see the hesitation in her eyes, knew she was weighing up things, knowing, too, that it could go either way at this point.

'You can tell me. I won't be shocked.'

'Shocked?' The hesitation disappeared and the sudden smile meant a decision had been reached and a confession was not on the cards. 'I'm worrying about nothing. Mike's going to be thrilled.'

Holding her, patting her back, murmuring comforting words, Christine, remembering the man in the bookshop, could only wonder and allow her suspicions to run riot.

Chapter Twenty

That very morning Amy and Mike were working together at the office.

Amy had spent the last few weeks going through the files that Shirley kept close to her chest. Everything was on computer, of course, paper files rapidly becoming a thing of the past, but it was interesting to look back at what had been happening this past year. There was nothing untoward, which she was glad about but Shirley did have her own peculiar system, which needed a little deciphering. When other people were not quite sure what was what, it meant that you kept control and that is precisely what Shirley had liked to do.

She had been the face of the company to some extent and Amy had to acknowledge with some reluctance that she would be missed. She had been wrong about Shirley; she had done her job well and that was a shock because it made her doubt her judgement where people were concerned. Her mother was just the same, making instant judgements about people, telling her later that she hadn't trusted Brian from the very beginning.

This was why she had not yet introduced her mother to Daniel. Christine kept asking and she knew that it had to come about sooner or later but she was desperate that her mother should like him. She wanted everybody to like him because she had long decided that he was the man she was going to spend the rest of her life with. She hesitated to tell anybody that yet and she wished that Janet was around because she was the one person she could have talked to about it.

'Fancy a spot of lunch?' Mike asked, stretching and yawning. He had already been here this morning when Amy arrived, looking bright and confident having got over the disappointment of the French connection that had apparently misfired big time.

'Why not?' She glanced at the clock. The lads from van one were off on a long-haul and the other lads were packing up one of the smaller vans for a short domestic. The order book was filling up, if not exactly full to bursting, and the new, much-improved website was up and running, resulting in a spate of inquiries that might or might not come to something. They were considering a new logo, a catchy slogan to go with it plus a batch of advertising but that was expensive and they needed to be sure the outlay would be worth it.

'How's Monique?' she asked as they set off to the Rose and Crown. She knew Mike so well that she anticipated that he would settle for the steak and ale pie and chips, with maybe some mushy peas on the side. She would probably be boringly healthy and go for a salad.

'She's fine,' he said guardedly. 'Although she's acting a bit like she's got jet-lag when she hasn't been on a plane.'

'She's probably not been sleeping very well, probably due to the disappointment about the cottage. I still can't believe that, Mike.'

'Neither can I. Her aunt was pulling a fast one, no two ways about it. Why would she show us that photograph of the wrong cottage if she wasn't trying to fool us? I can't understand it; she must have known that she would be found out as soon as Monique set eyes on it. It was an absolute shambles according to her. Roof caving in, mice living in it, damp and depressing, you name it.'

'That could be fixed,' Amy said carefully as he drove into the pub car park. 'It would cost money, true, but it would be worth it to get your dream place.'

'I don't think so. Structurally it's dodgy and you might as well just pull it down and start again. It's not just that. If it was just that we could consider it but she hates the village and we can't do a thing about that so it's best just to forget it. To tell the truth I was never convinced about the job I was offered. It was all a bit too vague for my liking and when I think about it we were damned fools to ever think it would work. You don't get given something for nothing in this life, Amy.'

They found a table inside, not easy because it was a popular place, and they studied the board for a minute before settling on exactly what Amy had predicted.

'How are you these days?' he asked returning to the table with their drinks, soft for both of them. 'You look good.'

'Thanks.' She smiled at him taking the glass of lime soda from him.

'And a bit different,' he added, peering at her with a brotherly interest. 'What's going on in your life? Still seeing that bloke?'

'Which one?' she asked cheekily as if she had two or three on the go.

He grinned at her and as he moved to pick up his glass the sun splintered through the window beside him and the whitened scar on his cheek glistened. She recalled the incident, the tantrum she had had and the heavy toy she threw at him, which had hit him and caused an instant rumpus, the cut deep so that a hasty trip to casualty was called for because it needed stitching.

'Did I ever say sorry about that scar?' she asked him now.

'What?' He put a hand up to his face, touched it. 'What are you talking about? Surely you're not still thinking about that? It was an accident, Amy, and accidents happen.'

'We should try to get on better together,' she told him.

'I don't know if you want to work with me and I wouldn't have come back if I hadn't thought that you were off to France. Now that you're not, though, maybe I should bow out gracefully.'

'And do what?' He asked in astonishment. 'God, Amy, you've given up your job and you've helped Mum a lot by moving in with her.'

'I'm not sure about that and it's not going to work long term. I thought it would but it's not easy to go back to being a teenager living at home. We neither of us fit into those roles anymore and it makes it awkward. Anyway, she's thinking of moving to something smaller and I'm thinking of moving in with my … friend,' she said, uncertain what to call Daniel. 'I know it might seem as if it's sudden but we've known each other for ages. We just didn't realize that we … ' she felt her cheeks flame. 'We like each other a lot,' she finished lamely.

'That's great news. I'm happy for you. Can I tell Monique? She'll be delighted but let's get one thing clear; you must not think that I don't want you working with me. We can do it, damn it, and we *should* do it for Dad's sake. He would be thrilled that you're on board and I want to show him … if he's up there … that he was wrong and that I can make a bloody good show of running things. Are you up for it? We can work together. I don't care about titles. You can be number one if you want.'

'I don't much care about titles either,' she said with a rueful smile. 'I have thought of a few ideas that can run with yours so let's not dismiss anything yet. Things will pick up but I think we can be doing a lot more to promote ourselves.'

'I'll leave that side of things to you,' he said, smiling at the waitress as their food arrived. 'And we can always call on that guy of yours if we need to.'

'Have you been checking up on me?' she asked, watching as he tucked into his pie. They were grown-ups, she reflected, and it was high time they behaved like grown-ups instead of it degenerating every single time into a children. 'How did you know what Daniel does for a living?'

'Mum told me,' he said innocently. 'It isn't meant to be a secret, is it? I think she's expecting great things of him. Why not bring him to meet us?'

She frowned, remembering the last time she brought somebody to meet them but that would not happen again, would it? One thing she knew for sure. If it had happened and Daniel had been present on Christmas Day, *he* would have never left her.

'We want you to be happy,' Mike said quietly. 'Honestly, Amy, that's all we want. And I want you to be as happy as I am with Monique. Married life has a lot going for it and she's just great. I know you two don't get on that well and I wish you would but believe me she's ... ' it was his turn to struggle and look embarrassed. 'Well, what can I say, sis? We intend to stay together for ever.'

'I know you do.' She made up her mind there and then to try harder. Monique was Monique and for better or worse, as sisters-in-law, they would be forever linked. Of course Monique had irritating little ways but then so did she.

Nobody was perfect although, just now, madly in love as she was with Daniel, he pretty much seemed so.

On her first visit, Christine ordered a book from the woman in the bookshop saying that she would pick it up when it came in.

She needed an excuse to see him again and she also wanted to see what his reaction would be when he realized just who she was, namely his lover's mother-in-law. She was now convinced that something was going on, had been going on for a while, and she was mortified that she had not seen through Monique. She might have voiced her suspicions to Frank if he had been alive although he would not have been the least surprised for he had always harboured doubts where his daughter-in-law was concerned.

How could she cheat on Mike? That man absolutely worshipped the ground she walked on and she had no business doing something that might hurt him. Resentment bubbled up on her son's behalf and she had no idea what she was going to do about it. She did not wish to confront Monique directly and although she had talked it over in a quiet moment with Oscar, the dog listening patiently, it had not helped. She did not feel she could talk about it with Amy because Amy would demand facts and there were no facts. It was all based on that most irrational of things; female intuition.

'She's sweeter than a can of syrup,' Frank had said after their first meeting with Monique and then, seeing Christine's annoyed face. 'Well, she is. I've met people like that before and they can't be trusted. I just can't believe she's as nice as she's making herself out to be. There has to be a bloody catch somewhere. I'll tell you one thing. She's going to run rings round him.'

'Frank Fletcher! They love each other. Can't you see that?' Her exasperation reached boiling point. Mike had brought this young woman to see them, a woman he plainly adored and this was what his father – in private – thought of her. It was, she saw, up to her to take Monique's corner.

And she had been doing it ever since.

A message left on her answerphone by the woman in the shop confirmed that the book she had ordered had arrived and was available for pick-up at her convenience. That morning before she left home she reached a decision. Following another discussion with Oscar, she determined what to do and that was to do absolutely nothing.

Female intuition was all very well but she was allowing her imagination to run riot here and all because of a foolish wrong number. She was still in that peculiar half-aware state that bereavement brings with it and had put two and two together to make a ridiculous number when she had nothing to go on except the alarmingly powerful sexual field given off by this other man, coupled with Monique's admitted worries about the pregnancy. She had assumed something, invented something, that was simply not correct and thank God she had not actually said what she had been thinking when consoling Monique. For a moment there she had nearly asked if the baby was definitely Mike's. The truth was that Monique's concerns were just the normal everyday worries of a woman in the early stages of her first pregnancy, that moment when you realized that there was no going back.

She would draw a line under all this nonsense. She would pick up the book from that shop, slip away and that would be that. She would leave the poor man alone and put a stop to the personal fantasizing about him. If she was ever to have a relationship again – and it was a very big if – then it would be with a man nearer her own age.

That was the plan and having made her mind up she made the bookshop her first port of call when she got into town.

Monique had told Mike the news and he was predictably delighted and already making plans for the future now that there were to be three of them. With the French move off, Christine suggested that they move in with Christine for the time being, which was eminently sensible. After some thought Christine had decided that a move to the village was premature and not something she should be doing at this stage.

'For the time being' had a sinister ring to it, though, and it was something they needed to discuss as a family. Christine was not old enough to be shunted into a granny flat on the premises; she was not even a grandmother as yet, and there was the eventual inheritance thing to think about and how it would affect Amy if they were lodged there.

'For heaven's sake, it's only until you can find something else,' Christine said to their doubts. 'I don't want you under my feet for long. The sooner you find something else the better but your buyers are starting to fret, aren't they; they're scared you're going to take it off the market and you don't want to do that, do you, because it's going to be a squeeze when the baby arrives. Make a decision, Mike.'

So he had and they were duly getting ready to vacate River Terrace and move into the Snape House.

There had been no communication recently from Sol. She needed to have one final meeting with him – out in the open with no sex this time – to inform him that it was over and they must not see each other ever again. It was going to be awkward with him living close by and she would have to tell him about the baby but she would not tell him that there was an even chance that he was the father. This baby was most definitely Mike's and the more she told herself that the more she believed it.

Sol was not answering his home number and she hesitated to ring him at the shop so it meant two visits to Lancaster; the first to drop a brief note – signed simply M – through his letter box giving a date and time and venue for their meeting and the second to actually turn up at the appointed time later that week in Williamson Park.

She knew now how spies must feel en route to an assignment as she made her way through the park towards the Ashton Memorial. There were few people about but then it was a chilly start to the day, dark clouds gathering overhead threatening a heavy downpour.

She was wearing a pale blue empire-line dress, perfect for early pregnancy, and a neat little cream cardigan with pearl buttons. Her flat shoes made no sound as she arrived a little early at the appointed place. On cue, the sun broke free of the clouds promising a few minutes of sunshine before it became hidden once more. She shook her hair free of its ribbon because Sol liked it that way, instantly wondering why she had done so; it hardly mattered any more what he thought.

The speech, the final goodbye, was rehearsed and she wanted to get it over with quickly without interruption. 'Hear me out,' she was going to say at the start and she would end by saying that she hoped he would understand and, if he loved her – if – then he would do the right thing and leave her alone from now on. There was to be no further contact.

She waited and the minutes ticked by.

After twenty long minutes she could wait no longer. The sun had long disappeared and spits of rain were starting to come down. She walked quickly back to her car and drove to his place, parking in the adjoining street as usual. She had a key to both the main door and his flat and she went up the stairs feeling guilty and hoping she didn't meet anybody. There was music blaring from one of the rooms on the first floor and she hurried past, standing a moment outside Sol's door and listening.

There was silence. She gave a tentative knock on the door and when there was no answer opened it.

Inside, it was empty.

The cheap furniture that came with it was still all there but she quickly saw that his personal stuff was gone.

'Hi there. It's up for rent again.' A young man stood in the doorway, from the flat below, earphones slung loosely round his neck, dyed red hair cut in a weird shape, face mottled with the after-effects of severe acne. 'The guy's gone. Pretty much did a runner. Here one day, gone the next.'

'Gone where?'

He shrugged. 'No idea. Can I help you? Did the agents give you a key?'

Thank goodness he didn't seem to know who she was but then in all the time she had been coming up here she had never once come across a soul.

She hesitated, needing to come up with a reason why she was here. 'It's too small,' she went on, standing now and offering him a wan smile. 'And there are too many stairs. I'll let them know.'

'Okay. I said I'd keep an eye on it. They're a sloppy lot, giving out keys to anybody. You're the fifth to visit.' He gave her an approving look. 'We're a happy bunch if you want to reconsider? I'm Paul. What's your name?'

'Are you Australian?' she asked avoiding answering the question.

'How did you guess?'

'I just did,' she said, adding quickly that she liked it just in case he took offence.

'We're a real mixed bunch here,' he said cheerfully as they returned to the hall where a bike was propped up against the wall next to a heap of coats. 'That guy up there wasn't a student. Older bloke. Kept himself to himself. Mind you, he did have a visitor from time to time. Good-looking blonde apparently.' He opened the front door, let her pass.

She caught the amused look in his eyes, knew annoyingly that he *knew*. She had not fooled him for a minute.

Very aware of his eyes on her, she walked away.

Days earlier, Christine's best laid plans took a tumble the minute she walked into the shop and saw Solomon Diamond behind the counter. What were the chances of that name being his real one?

'You have a book for me,' she told him as he stood to greet her.

There was a pile of supposedly reserved books on the shelf behind him and he went over to them asking for her name and contact number.

And then, as he retrieved her book, unable to stop herself she came right out with it.

'I believe you know my daughter-in-law Monique,' she said with a smile. 'She's told me all about you.'

'She has?' He returned her smile uncertainly. 'Well, yes, we know each other from way back. We were at school together and then we went off to the same art college.' The hesitation was brief but noticeable. 'How is she these days?'

'Pregnant,' she said in a low voice. 'Have you time for a coffee, Mr Diamond? I think we need to talk.'

'About what?' His smile was unrepentant. 'But I'll have a coffee with you if you like. We'll go to the café up the road.'

Sometimes it was best to be honest, to address your fears, and Christine had no need to resort to stretching him on the rack for him to come up with a confession. Without much persuasion, seeing her face, he admitted to a bit of a fling, but Monique loved her husband and it had meant nothing and no, it would not happen again.

'You bet it won't, Mr Diamond,' she told him as they sat at a table by the window with their lattes. It was a jolt to know that Frank had been right all along and a severe blow to know that her suspicions had been correct. All she knew was that it would kill Mike if he ever found out. 'Are you staying around here for the foreseeable future because I think it might be a very good idea if you moved away?'

'You don't beat about the bush, do you, Christine?'

She felt her heart give a little leap. Goodness, there was something fascinating about him, such a promise in those eyes, even a hint of interest in *her*, which she was quick to pick up on and she could understand Monique falling for the charm even if she could scarcely condone it. She had been tempted once or twice during her own long marriage but she was a Catholic by birth and nurture and her marriage vows meant something to her. Now, of course, she was free again but having a fling with this man was out of the question. Looking at him calmly, meeting his gaze, she knew that she had to assert herself and quickly before she gave out any more confusing signals.

'How attached are you to your business, Mr Diamond?'

she persisted. 'How much would it take for you to leave town?'

His laugh rang out. 'For Christ's sake, woman, what film are we in? Are you trying to bribe me now?'

'I don't want to see my son hurt,' she explained, glancing round to see if they were being observed and deciding that nobody was remotely interested in them. 'I am a mother and a mother will do a lot to protect her child no matter how old that child is. Name a figure and I'll see what I can do but you then have to remove yourself and quickly. I'll leave you to dispose of your business.' She stopped, appalled at her own audacity, knowing even as she said it that she was asking an awful lot of him, too much, maybe.

It was also going to cost her.

There was a long silence whilst he toyed with the spoon in his saucer. She could hardly believe she had done this, offered him a bribe, and it was so daft that she half expected him to laugh at her and walk out.

'Okay. No problem there.' He shrugged, a smile still playing lightly around his lips. 'I don't want your money, Christine Fletcher, but I will leave town if that's what you want. As for the business, I'll be glad to see the back of it; my assistant's wanted to take it over for years.'

'Well, then ... there's nothing to stop you, is there?'

'I don't want us to have secrets,' Daniel told her over breakfast.

Amy was already making plans for doing up his place. Redecorating was high on the agenda and she had already bought a few bits and bobs to add a bit of interest. She had moved all her stuff in, except for the boxes of treasures that still lay up in the loft at Snape House; she was sure her mother wouldn't mind storing them for her a while longer.

'That sounds ominous,' she said, glancing at the clock because even though they were still in the throes of that wonderful honeymoon period – without the getting married bit – she needed to get into work. 'Have we time for this now?'

'I wasn't quite truthful when it came to Beatrice,' he said with a rueful smile. 'We did have a thing going and I think that she would have liked it to continue but I had second thoughts. You know why?'

'Because you suddenly realized you were head in heels in love with me?' she said. 'Look, it doesn't matter because I've had my share of other men. Not many,' she added hastily as she caught his smile. 'Just a few.'

'Janet did tell me about the last one.'

'Honestly.' She clicked her tongue. 'She had no business to do that but then I suppose she was just concerned about me. I must drop her a line, find out how she is.'

'I've done that already and she's absolutely fine. So, let's draw a line under the Beatrice thing, shall we?'

'It's already forgotten and if I don't get a move on, I'm going to be last in and I don't like that. And nor does Mike. I'm going to be an aunt, by the way, which will make you an uncle!'

'Great. She can be a flower girl when we get married. Or if she's a boy he can be a page. What do you think?'

'I think,' she grabbed a piece of toast, 'that if that was a proposal you've picked a very bad moment. Got to go.' She kissed him and he held her close a moment.

'I've got to go,' she repeated, glancing ruefully at her blouse. 'Look at this. I've got butter on it and I haven't time to change.'

'I love you, Amy,' he said.

'I love you, too, and it's a yes by the way.' Ducking away from him, she grabbed her bag and jacket, blowing him a kiss on the way out.

Chapter Twenty One

Christine was babysitting, giving Monique a break. Come to think of it, she was always giving Monique a break. She dared not voice it, not to herself and certainly not to Mike but Monique was a bit lackadaisical when it came to the child. There was no doubt that she loved him, in her way, but she did not actually show it very often. Her maternal instincts, if not entirely non-existent were sadly on the low side, and she was more than happy to hand him over to Christine at any opportunity.

Wasn't this exactly what she had once wished for? Of course she was thrilled with him and delighted in looking after him but she did wish Monique would show a little more responsibility, for after all she was his mother. She was also beginning to regret the day she had offered them a home at Snape House; they showed no signs of wanting to move out and why should they when her presence made it so convenient for Monique to pursue her life unhindered by her child?

She had said in her Christmas note this year what a good mother Monique was but then she always exaggerated the positive in those notes. This year, though, she had been perfectly truthful when she said how well Mike was running the business in the absence of his father. And she had no need to exaggerate how happy Amy was these days for it was plain to see.

As for baby Alexander looking like his father, well that was absolutely true, too.

She heard Mike's car, peeped through the window and saw him lifting out the tree. Good. She would decorate it this afternoon with Monique, who had offered to help. Despite her new-found reservations about her daughter-in-law she was determined to keep their relationship intact, although ironically, just as that had subtly changed over the past year, so had the one between the sisters-in-law. It was so much better these days although that could be something to do with the fact that Amy had finally found love and was much more relaxed. The other day, for instance, she had walked in on the pair of them and found them giggling together like schoolgirls. Amy loved little Alexander to bits and in the absence of a surfeit of mummy-cuddling she and Amy between them provided more than enough.

For a minute, she thought of Frank as she opened the box of Christmas decorations that she had got down from the loft, stuff the kids had made. It would please Frank that the tree this year would look a little more lived-in if a shade less elegant. Seeing her sitting on the floor, Oscar came bounding over to sit beside her and she stroked his soft furry head. Alexander was starting to grumble and she stood up and went over, picking him up at once, cuddling him and planting a kiss on top of his baby head with its soft brown curls.

It would be hard this year, especially on Boxing Day, but they would cope as a family and see it through and this year Amy would have proper support from Daniel, a man of whom she thoroughly approved. She had not approved of him *too* much in case in some perverse way she somehow put her daughter off him but you only had to look at them to see that they were head over heels in love.

She would not breathe a word to Mike about his wife's affair – that was a closed book – and even though she had been sorely tempted to tell Monique the truth surrounding Solomon Diamond's sudden departure, there were some things best left unsaid.

The business was slowly creeping up again with some of Mike's ideas bearing fruit and he was relishing the opportunity presented to him, just as, years ago, Frank had also relished it. It was tragic that Frank had to die in order for Mike to show them what he was made of but some day when and if they met up again, she would take great pleasure in telling her husband how wrong he had been.

'Bloody Christmas trees!' Mike said with feeling, carrying it into the room. 'I'm scratched to ribbons. I don't know why we bother.'

'We bother because it's tradition and don't be grumpy,' she told him, feeling the excitement that the first sight and pine smell of the tree caused. 'Stick it in the corner. Monique's going to help with the decorations later and Amy's coming over as well.'

'Are you sure you're okay, Mum?' he asked following her into the kitchen where preparations were in full swing; everybody would be here this evening for a pre-Christmas meal. 'I know it's going to be tough. We wouldn't mind, you know, if you wanted to abandon it this year.'

'Abandon Christmas? Absolutely not,' she said. 'I wouldn't dream of it. We have Alexander now and he will keep us busy and take our minds off it.'

He was gone. Sol was gone.

Monique wondered if she would ever have got round to finishing it between them, but he had saved her the bother by disappearing. And now she had Alexander who looked like *her* and everybody said what a sweet baby he was.

She had got away with it and sometimes she looked at Alexander and could see Mike.

The trouble was she could sometimes see Sol, too.

She loved Alexander, of course, but her aunt was right

for the females in her family were strangely disinterested in children so it was just as well that Mike and the rest of the Fletchers all fussed over him in a way that quite bewildered her. Perhaps it would be better when he was older and she could hold a reasonable conversation with him.

Babies, in her eyes, were grossly overrated creatures.

A few days before Christmas, Christine spent the afternoon decorating the tree. Monique helped her, pretty in pink, her slim figure regained and looking at her Christine suddenly realized that she was over it, that her daughter-in-law had made her decision to stay firmly in the fold of this family so nothing more needed to be said. There was an awkward moment following Solomon's disappearance when she had seemed withdrawn but that moment passed and when the baby was born and everybody instantly remarked how like Monique he looked she captured the relief in her daughter-in-law's face.

Yet Monique was Monique and because the maternal gene seemed to have bypassed her, Christine felt a grandmotherly responsibility to ensure that Alexander did not miss out on love, although with a father who doted on him and an aunt who likewise thought the sun shone out of him and her own protective instincts on high alert there was no danger of that. Alexander was very like Monique, although the dark brown curls that were starting to appear were a worry, but yesterday for the first time she had caught something in his eyes that reminded her so much of Mike.

Or was that wishful thinking? Whether or not Alexander was her true grandchild was of no consequence because she had already developed a bond with him and she would keep the secret to her grave.

The fairy lights were the final touch to the tree, the *pièce de résistance*. Christine tackled the fickle Christmas lights, hastily put away last year in a very higgledy-piggledy fashion so that they were tangled to high heaven and, with Monique's help, the two of them laughing helplessly, untangled them at last and draped them all around the tree. It was exhausting work, the needles were sharp and the childish decorations did not marry particularly well with the expensive and delicate silver ornaments of last year but she was finally ready to switch them on.

'Right. We're ready to go. I'm going to switch them on, Mike,' she called. 'Come through, everybody.'

They gathered round and she handed round glasses of champagne, for with Amy newly engaged to be married they had something to celebrate. The tree looked beautiful standing by the window. It was growing dark outside with sadly no sign of the snowflakes of last year.

'Are we taking bets on whether they work or not?' Mike asked, holding the baby and pointing out the tree to him. 'It'll be a miracle if they do.'

She caught her breath for he was not to know those were his father's very words at the same moment last year.

'Of course they'll work. Have faith,' she told him, returning his smile. 'Fingers crossed everybody. Your father ...' she gulped as emotion flooded through her, 'he usually did a countdown. Shall we?'

'For heaven's sake, are we completely mad?' Amy laughed up at Daniel. 'I hope you know what you're letting yourself in for coming into this family?'

'I certainly do.' Daniel put his arm round her and raised his glass. 'Cheers, everybody.'

'Cheers!'

With Oscar catching their excitement and giving a little bark, Christine flicked the switch.